Anonymous

Roses and Holly

A Gift-Book for All the Year

Anonymous

Roses and Holly
A Gift-Book for All the Year

ISBN/EAN: 9783337417727

Printed in Europe, USA, Canada, Australia, Japan

Cover: Foto ©Andreas Hilbeck / pixelio.de

More available books at **www.hansebooks.com**

ROSES AND HOLLY:

A GIFT-BOOK FOR ALL THE YEAR.

WITH ORIGINAL ILLUSTRATIONS

BY

GOURLAY STEELL, R.S.A.   *SAMUEL BOUGH, A.R.S.A.*
R. HERDMAN, R.S.A.   *JOHN M'WHIRTER, A.R.S.A.*
CLARK STANTON, A.R.S.A.   *JOHN LAWSON.*
AND OTHER EMINENT ARTISTS.
ENGRAVED BY R. PATERSON.

EDINBURGH:
WILLIAM P. NIMMO.

PRINTED BY BALLANTYNE AND COMPANY
EDINBURGH AND LONDON

PREFACE.

WE have ventured to name this pictorial and literary treasury,
ROSES AND HOLLY. The rose—the queen of flowers—is
significant of summer, of beauty, and of love: the holly—the ever-
green of happiness—which cheers the heart through the gloom of
winter, and shadows round the Christmas hearth pleasant memo-
ries, and feelings of friendship, of comfort, and of gaiety. The
two ends of the year meet in these emblematic flowers ; and, with
a liberty which we hope will not be too closely questioned, we
have chosen them as the appellation of our Gift Book for all the
Year.

In preparing ROSES AND HOLLY, the idea of the editor has
been to depart in some measure from the beaten track of his pre-
decessors. Instead of the classified selections and special subjects
which are usually chosen for Gift Books, and to which all due
credit for excellence of taste and propriety of judgment is heartily
awarded, it seemed to him that a miscellaneous collection of art
and literary gems, grouped together "in most admired disorder,"
would form a volume of interest and value.

The main object kept in view in the preparation of ROSES AND
HOLLY has been to secure variety in the selection ; while literary

merit, it need scarcely be added, has not been overlooked in the articles chosen. In the volume will be found poetry for the imaginative, and prose for the matter-of-fact ; matter serious and didactic for the reflective : mirth for the merry : in the words of the dramatist—

"There's no want of meat, sir ;
Portly and curious viands are prepared,
To please all kinds of appetites."

The illustrations which adorn ROSES AND HOLLY have been specially drawn and engraved for the volume ; and among them will be found original examples of several of the most distinguished Scottish artists. The entire artistic and mechanical work has been executed in the Northern Capital ; and the publisher puts it forth with some degree of confidence, as a favourable example of art and typography.

ILLUSTRATIONS,

ENGRAVED BY R. PATERSON.

CONTENTS.

CONTENTS.

Of Roses sweet and Holly leaves so bright :
  Of Summer's charm and Winter's pleasant flower;
  This page is compass'd in a floral bower.
Here, traced by cunning hand of art's high light,
The Seasons, wreathed in Love and Joy, unite.
  Of Love, the god himself his presence lends,
  And Joy, o'er all her fragrant sweetness blends,
To aid enjoyment and increase delight.
" Roses and Holly !"   The year's antipodes !
  The Summer's sunshine and the Winter's glow—
Spring's opening day, and Autumn's fruitfulness—
  The cycle of the Seasons here below,
This wreath doth show.   May it ne'er fail to prove
A heart's tribute to friendship and to love !

SPRING.

SWEETLY breathing vernal air,
    That with kind warmth dost repair,
Winter's ruins, from whose breast
All the gums and spice of th' east
Borrow their perfumes ; whose eye
Gilds the morn, and clears the sky ;
Whose dishevell'd tresses shed
Pearls upon the violet bed ;
On whose brow, with calm smiles drest,
The halcyon sits, and builds her nest ;
Beauty, youth, and endless spring,
Dwell upon thy rosy wing !

Thou, if stormy Boreas throws
Down whole forests when he blows,
With a pregnant flowery birth
Canst refresh the teaming earth.
If he nip the early bud,
If he blast what 's fair or good,
If he scatter our choice flowers,
If he shake our hall or bowers,
If his rude breath threaten us,
Thou canst stroke great Æolus,
And from him the grace obtain
To bind him in an iron chain.

Carew.

A CLUSTER OF SHAKESPEARIAN PROVERBS.

TRUE hope is swift, and flies with swallow's wings.
Every subject's duty is the king's, but every subject's soul is his own.
One touch of nature makes the whole world kin.
Cowards die many times before their deaths.
Praising what is lost, makes the remembrance dear.
The devil can cite Scripture for his purpose.
All things that are, are with more spirit chased and enjoyed.
He is well paid that is well satisfied.
An honest tale speeds best.
Every one can master a grief, but he that hath it.
Spirits are not finely touched, but to fine issues.
The ripest fruit first falls.
He jests at scars that never felt a wound.
What wound did ever heal but by degrees?
Poor and content is rich, and rich enough.
The labour we delight in physics pain.
Thrice is he armed, that hath his quarrel just.
Tell truth and shame the devil.
Things without all remedy should be without regard.
Virtue is bold, and goodness never fearful.
Suspicion always haunts the guilty mind.
A woman's reason: I think him so, because I think him so.
Make a virtue of necessity.
What stronger breastplate than a heart untainted!
The thief doth fear each bush an officer.
The sight of means to do ill-deeds, makes ill-deeds done.
Sweet are the uses of adversity.
We that are true lovers, run into strange capers.
He that wants money, means, and content, is without three good friends.
Frailty, thy name is woman.
A dream itself is but a shadow.
The devil hath power to assume a pleasing shape.
Words without thoughts never to heaven go.

WHAT IS WIT?

IT is indeed a thing so versatile and multiform, appearing in so many shapes, so many postures, so many garbs, so variously apprehended by several eyes and judgments, that it seemeth no less hard to settle a clear and certain notion thereof, than to make a portrait of Proteus, or to define the figure of a fleeting air. Sometimes it lieth in pat allusion to a known story, or in seasonable application of a trivial saying, or in forging an apposite tale : sometimes it playeth in words and phrases, taking advantage from the ambiguity of their sense, or the affinity of their sound : sometimes it is wrapped in a dress of humorous expression : sometimes it lurketh under an odd similitude : sometimes it is lodged in a sly question, in a smart answer, in a quirkish reason, in a shrewd imitation, in cunningly diverting or cleverly retorting an objection : sometimes it is couched in a bold scheme of speech, in a tart irony, in a lusty hyperbole, in a startling metaphor, in a plausible reconciling of contradictions, or in acute nonsense : sometimes a scenical representation of persons or things, a counterfeit speech, a mimical look or gesture passeth for it : sometimes an affected simplicity, sometimes a presumptuous bluntness, giveth it being : sometimes it riseth from a lucky hitting upon what is strange, sometimes from a crafty wresting obvious matter to the purpose : often it consisteth in one knows not what, and springeth up one can hardly tell how. Its ways are unaccountable and inexplicable, being answerable to the numberless rovings of fancy and windings of language. It is, in short, a manner of speaking out of the simple and plain way, (such as reason teacheth and proveth things by,) which, by a pretty surprising uncouthness in conceit or expression, doth affect and amuse the fancy, stirring in it some wonder, and breeding some delight thereto.   *Barrow.*

YOUNG AUTHORS.

THE excitement of literary composition pretty soon subsides with the hired labourer, and the delight of seeing one's self in print only extends to the first two or three appearances in the magazine or newspaper page. Pegasus put into harness, and obliged to run a stage every day, is as prosaic as any other hack, and won't work without his whip or his feed of corn.   *Thackeray.*

A CLUSTER OF GERMAN PROVERBS.

BY the street of Bye-and-By one arrives at the house of Never.
With great men one must allow five to be an even number.
If you are an anvil, be patient; if you are a hammer, strike hard.
Wait is a hard word for the hungry.
War is pleasant to those who have not tried it.
One to-day is better than ten to-morrows.
There are only two good women in the world: one is dead, and the other cannot be found.
" I have" is a better bird than " If I had."
Neutrals think to tread on eggs and break none.
Disputing and borrowing cause grief and sorrowing.
" Your words are fair," said the wolf, " but I will not come into the village."
Once in people's mouths, 'tis hard to get out of them.

A CLUSTER OF SPANISH PROVERBS.

WITH a staircase before you, you look for a rope to go down by.
If you have a loitering servant, set his dinner before him and send him on an errand.
A peasant between two lawyers is like a fish between two cats.
In a smith's house the knife is wooden.
In a country of the blind, the one-eyed is king.
What is mine is my own; my brother Juan's is his and mine.
He is a fool who thinks that another does not think.
There's no argument like that of the stick.
Words will not do for my aunt; she has not faith even in deeds.
When God pleases it rains in fair weather.
A secret between two is God's secret: a secret between three is every body's.
The earth hides as it takes the physician's mistakes.

THE GIANT AND THE DWARF.

NCE upon a time, a Giant and a Dwarf were friends, and kept together. They made a bargain that they would never forsake each other, but go seek adventures. The first battle they fought was with two Saracens, and the Dwarf, who was very courageous, dealt one of the champions a most angry blow. It did the Saracen but very little injury, who, lifting up his sword, fairly struck off the poor Dwarf's arm. He was now in a woeful plight; but the Giant coming to his assistance, in a short time left the two Saracens dead on the plain, and the Dwarf cut off the dead man's head out of spite. They then travelled on to another adventure. This was against three bloody-minded Satyrs, who were carrying away a damsel in distress. The Dwarf was not quite so fierce now as before; but for all that, struck the first blow; which was returned by another, that knocked out his eye: but the Giant was soon up with them, and had they not fled, would certainly have killed them every one. They were all very joyful for this victory, and the damsel who was relieved fell in love with the Giant, and married him. They now travelled far, and farther than I can tell, till they met with a company of robbers. The Giant, for the first time, was foremost now; but the Dwarf was not far behind. The battle was stout and long. Wherever the Giant came, all fell before him; but the Dwarf had like to have been killed more than once. At last the victory declared for the two adventurers: but the Dwarf lost his leg. The Dwarf had now lost an arm, a leg, and an eye, while the Giant was without a single wound. Upon which he cried out to his little companion: " My little hero, this is glorious sport; let us get one victory more, and then we shall have honour for ever." " No," cries the Dwarf, who was by this time grown wiser— " no, I declare off; I 'll fight no more; for I find in every battle that you get all the honour and rewards, but all the blows fall upon me."

Goldsmith.

THE LOVE OF COUNTRY AND OF HOME.

THERE is a land, of every land the pride,
  Beloved by Heaven, o'er all the world beside ;
Where brighter suns dispense serener light,
And milder moons emparadise the night ;
A land of beauty, virtue, valour, truth,
Time-tutor'd age, and love-exalted youth :
The wandering mariner, whose eye explores
The wealthiest isles, the most enchanting shores,
Views not a realm so bountiful and fair,
Nor breathes the spirit of a purer air ;
In every clime the magnet of his soul,
Touch'd by remembrance, trembles to that pole ;
For in this land of Heaven's peculiar grace,
The heritage of nature's noblest race,
There is a spot of earth supremely blest,
A dearer, sweeter spot than all the rest :
Where man, creation's tyrant, casts aside
His sword and sceptre, pageantry and pride,
While in his soften'd looks benignly blend
The sire, the son, the husband, father, friend :
Here woman reigns ; the mother, daughter, wife,
Strews with fresh flowers the narrow way of life ;
In the clear heaven of her delightful eye,
An angel-guard of loves and graces lie ;
Around her knees domestic duties meet,
And fireside pleasures gambol at her feet.
" Where shall that *land*, that *spot of earth* be found ? "
Art thou a man *?*—a patriot ?—look around ;
Oh, thou shalt find, howe'er thy footsteps roam,
That land THY COUNTRY, and that spot THY HOME !

Montgomery.

THE THEORY OF QUARRELLING.

Touchstone. I did dislike the cut of a certain courtier's beard; he sent me word, if I said his beard was not cut well, he was in the mind it was : this is called the *Retort courteous.* If I sent him word, again, it was not well cut, he would send me word, he cut it to please himself : this is called the *Quip modest.* If again, it was not well cut, he disabled my judgment : this is called the *Reply churlish.* If again, it was not well cut, he would answer, I spake not true : this is called the *Reproof valiant.* If again, it was not well cut, he would say I lie : this is called the *Countercheck quarrelsome :* and so to the *Lie circumstantial,* and the *Lie direct.*

Jaques. And how oft did you say his beard was not well cut ?

Touchstone. I durst go no further than the *Lie circumstantial,* nor he durst not give me the *Lie direct ;* and so we measured swords, and parted.

Jaques. Can you nominate in order now the degrees of the lie ?

Touchstone. O Sir, we quarrel in print, by the book ; as you have books for good manners : I will name you the degrees. The first, the Retort courteous ; the second, the Quip modest ; the third, the Reply churlish ; the fourth, the Reproof valiant ; the fifth, the Countercheck quarrelsome ; the sixth, the Lie with circumstance ; the seventh, the Lie direct. All these you may avoid, but the Lie direct ; and you may avoid that too, with an "if." I knew when seven justices could not take up a quarrel : but when the parties were met themselves, one of them thought but of an "if," as "If you said so, then I said so ;" and they shook hands, and swore brothers. Your "if" is the only peacemaker ; much virtue in "if."

Shakespeare.

THE NOBILITY OF AMBITION.

AMBITION is the stamp impress'd by Heaven
     To mark the noblest minds; with active heat
Inform'd, they mount the precipice of power,
Grasp at command, and tower in quest of empire ;
While vulgar souls compassionate their cares,
Gaze at their height and tremble at their danger.
Thus meaner spirits with amazement mark
The varying seasons, and revolving skies,
And ask, what guilty power's rebellious hand
Rolls with eternal toil the pond'rous orbs?
While some archangel, nearer to perfection,
In easy state presides o'er all their motions,
Directs the planets with a careless nod,
Conducts the sun, and regulates the spheres.

Johnson.

THE HEIGHT OF HONOUR.

NO man to offend—
Ne'er to reveal the secrets of a friend ;
Rather to suffer, than to do a wrong.
To make the heart no stranger to the tongue ;
Provoked, not to betray an enemy.
Nor at his meat I choke with flattery;
Blushless to tell wherefore I wear my scars,
Or for my conscience, or my country's wars ;
To aim at just things, if we've wildly run
Into offences, wish them all undone,
'Tis poor, in grief for a wrong done, to die,
Honour to dare to live, and satisfy.

Massinger.

A GOOD WORD FOR PUBLISHERS.

" I PROTEST against that wretch of a middle-man whom I see between Genius and his great landlord, the Public, and who stops more than half of the labourer's earnings and fame."

"I am a prose labourer," Warrington said : "you, my boy, are a poet in a small way, and so, I suppose, consider you are authorised to be flighty. What is it you want? Do you want a body of capitalists that shall be forced to purchase the works of all authors, who may present themselves, manuscript in hand? Everybody who writes his epic, every driveller who can or can't spell, and produces his novel or his tragedy,—are they all to come and find a bag of sovereigns in exchange for their worthless reams of paper? Who is to settle what is good or bad, saleable or otherwise? Will you give the buyer leave, in fine, to purchase or not? Why, sir, when Johnson sate behind the screen at Saint John's Gate, and took his dinner apart, because he was too shabby and poor to join the literary bigwigs who were regaling themselves round Mr Cave's best table-cloth, the tradesman was doing him no wrong. You couldn't force the publisher to recognise the man of genius in the young man who presented himself before him, ragged, gaunt, and hungry. Rags are not a proof of genius ; whereas capital is absolute, as times go, and is perforce the bargain-master. It has a right to deal with the literary inventor as with any other ;—if I produce a novelty in the book trade, I must do the best I can with it ; but I can no more force Mr Murray to purchase my book of travels or sermons, than I can compel Mr Tattersall to give me a hundred guineas for my horse. I may have my own ideas of the value of my Pegasus, and think him the most wonderful of animals ; but the dealer has a right to his opinion, too, and may want a lady's horse, or a cob for a heavy timid rider, or a sound hack for the road, and my beast won't suit him."   *Thackeray.*

L'ALLEGRO.

COME, thou goddess fair and free,
   In heaven yclep'd Euphrosyne,
And by men heart-easing Mirth,
Whom lovely Venus, at a birth,
With two sister Graces more,
To ivy-crownèd Bacchus bore:
Or whether (as some sages sing)
The frolic wind that breathes the spring,
Zephyr, with Aurora playing,
As he met her once a-Maying,
There, on beds of violets blue,
And fresh-blown roses wash'd in dew,
Fill'd her with thee, a daughter fair,
So buxom, blithe, and debonair.
   Haste thee, nymph, and bring with thee
Jest, and youthful jollity,
Quips, and cranks, and wanton wiles,
Nods, and becks, and wreathèd smiles,
Such as hang on Hebe's cheek,
And love to live in dimple sleek;
Sport that wrinkled Care derides,
And Laughter holding both his sides.
Come, and trip it, as you go,
On the light fantastic toe;
And in thy right hand lead with thee
The mountain nymph, sweet Liberty:
And, if I give thee honour due,
Mirth, admit me of thy crew,
To live with her, and live with thee,
In unreprovèd pleasures free:

To hear the lark begin his flight,
And, singing, startle the dull night,
From his watch-tower in the skies,
Till the dappled dawn doth rise ;
Then to come, in spite of sorrow,
And at my window bid good-morrow,
Through the sweetbrier, or the vine,
Or the twisted eglantine :
While the cock, with lively din,
Scatters the rear of darkness thin,
And to the stack, or the barn-door,
Stoutly struts his dames before :
Oft listening how the hounds and horn
Cheerly rouse the slumbering morn,
From the side of some hoar hill,
Through the high wood echoing shrill ;
Some time walking, not unseen,
By hedgerow elms, on hillocks green,
Right against the eastern gate
Where the great sun begins his state,
Robed in flames, and amber light,
The clouds in thousand liveries dight ;
While the ploughman, near at hand,
Whistles o'er the furrow'd land,
And the milkmaid singeth blithe,
And the mower whets his scythe,
And every shepherd tells his tale,
Under the hawthorn in the dale.
　　Straight mine eye hath caught new pleasures,
Whilst the landscape round it measures ;
Russet lawns, and fallows gray,
Where the nibbling flocks do stray ;
Mountains, on whose barren breast
The labouring clouds do often rest ;
Meadows trim, with daisies pied,
Shallow brooks and rivers wide ;

Towers and battlements it sees
Bosom'd high in tufted trees,
Where, perhaps, some beauty lies,
The cynosure of neighbouring eyes.
   Hard by, a cottage chimney smokes
From betwixt two agèd oaks,
Where Corydon and Thyrsis met,
Are at their savoury dinner set
Of herbs, and other country messes,
Which the neat-handed Phillis dresses:
And then in haste her bower she leaves,
With Thestylis to bind the sheaves;
Or, if the earlier season lead,
To the tann'd haycock in the mead.
   Sometimes, with secure delight,
The upland hamlets will invite,
When the merry bells ring round,
And the jocund rebecks sound
To many a youth and many a maid
Dancing in the checker'd shade;
And young and old come forth to play
On a sunshine holiday,
Till the livelong daylight fail:
Then to the spicy nut-brown ale,
With stories told of many a feat,
How fairy Mab the junkets eat:
She was pinch'd, and pull'd, she said;
And he, by friar's lantern led,
Tells how the drudging goblin sweat
To earn his cream-bowl duly set
When, in one night, ere glimpse of morn,
His shadowy flail hath thresh'd the corn,
That ten day-labourers could not end;
Then lies him down the lubber fiend,
And, stretch'd out all the chimney's length,
Basks at the fire his hairy strength:

And, crop-full, out of doors he flings,
Ere the first cock his matin rings.
Thus done the tales, to bed they creep,
By whispering winds soon lull'd asleep.
  Tower'd cities please us then,
And the busy hum of men,
Where throngs of knights and barons bold,
In weeds of peace, high triumphs hold,
With store of ladies, whose bright eyes
Rain influence, and judge the prize
Of wit or arms, while both contend
To win her grace, whom all commend.
There let Hymen oft appear
In saffron robe, with taper clear,
And pomp, and feast, and revelry,
With mask and antique pageantry;
Such sights as youthful poets dream
On summer eves by haunted stream.
Then to the well-trod stage anon,
If Jonson's learnèd sock be on,
Or sweetest Shakespeare, Fancy's child,
Warble his native wood-notes wild.
  And ever, against eating cares,
Lap me in soft Lydian airs,
Married to immortal verse,
Such as the meeting soul may pierce,
In notes, with many a winding bout
Of linkèd sweetness long drawn out,
With wanton heed and giddy cunning,
The melting voice through mazes running,
Untwisting all the chains that tie
The hidden soul of harmony;
That Orpheus' self may heave his head,
From golden slumber on a bed
Of heap'd Elysian flowers, and hear
Such strains as would have won the ear

Of Pluto, to have quite set free
His half-regain'd Eurydice.
These delights if thou canst give,
Mirth, with thee I mean to live.

Milton.

THE ISLAND.

I F the author of the Irish Melodies had ever had a little isle so much
his own as I have possessed, he might not have found it so sweet as
the song anticipates. It has been my fortune, like Robinson Crusoe, to
be thrown on such a desolate spot; and I felt so lonely, though I had a
follower, that I wish *Moore* had been there. I had the honour of being in
that tremendous action off Finisterre, which proved the end of the earth
to many a brave fellow. I was ordered with a boarding party forcibly to
enter the Santissima Trinidada : but in the act of climbing into the quar-
ter-gallery, which, however, gave no quarter, was rebutted by the but-end
of a gun—a marine's ; who remained the quarter-master of the place. I
fell senseless into the sea, and should no doubt have perished in the
waters of oblivion, but for the kindness of John Monday, who picked me
up to go adrift with him in one of the ship's boats. All our oars were
carried away,—that is to say, we did not carry away any oars ; and while
shot was raining, our feeble hailing was unheeded. As may be supposed,
our boat was anything but the jolly-boat ; for we had no provisions to
spare in the middle of an immense waste. We were, in fact, adrift in the
cutter, with nothing to cut. We had not even junk for junketing, and
nothing but salt-water, even if the wind should blow fresh. Famine indeed
seemed to stare each of us in the face,—that is, we stared at one another.
We were truly in a very disagreeable pickle, with oceans of brine and no
beef ; and, I fancy, we would have exchanged a pound of gold for a pound
of flesh. No bread rose in the east, and in the opposite point we were
equally disappointed. We could not compass a meal any how, but got
mealy-mouthed, notwithstanding.

Time hung heavy on our hands, for our fast days seemed to pass very
slowly ; and our strength was rapidly sinking, from being so much afloat.
Still we nourished Hope, though we had nothing to give her. But at last
we lost all prospect of land, if one may say so when no land was in sight.
The weather got thicker as we were getting thinner ; and though we kept
a sharp watch, it was a very bad look-out. We could see nothing before
us but nothing to eat and drink. At last the fog cleared off, and we saw
something like land right head : but, alas ! the wind was in our teeth as

well as in our stomachs. We could do nothing but "keep her near," and
as we could not keep ourselves full, we luckily suited the course of the
boat; so that, after a tedious beating about—for the wind not only gives
blows, but takes a great deal of beating—we came to an island. Here we
landed, and our first impulse on coming to dry land was to drink. There
was a little brook at hand, to which we applied ourselves, till it seemed
actually to murmur at our inordinate thirst. Our next care was to look for
some food; for though our hearts were full at our escape, the neighbouring region was dreadfully empty. We succeeded in getting some natives
out of their bed, but with difficulty got them open; a common oyster-knife
would have been worth the price of a sceptre. Our next concern was to
look out for a lodging; and at last we discovered an empty cave, reminding
me of an old inscription at Portsmouth, "The hole of this place is to let."
We took the precaution of rolling some great stones to the entrance, for
fear of last lodgers,—lest some bear might come home from business, or a
tiger to tea. Here, under the rock, we slept without rocking; and when,
through the night's failing, the day broke, we saw, with the first instalment
of light, that we were upon a small desert isle, now for the first time an
Isle of Man.   *Hood.*

THE ADVANTAGES OF TRAVELLING.

IT draws the grossness off the understanding,
   And renders active and industrious spirits.
He that knows most men's manners must of necessity
Best know his own, and mend those, by example.
'Tis a dull thing to travel like a mill horse,
Still in the place he was born in, lamed and blinded;
Living at home is like it. Pure and strong spirits,
That, like the fire, still covet to fly upward,
And to give fire, as well as take it, eased up and mew'd here
I mean at home, like lusty-mettled horses,
Only tied up in stables to please their masters,
Beat out their fiery lives in their own litters.
                                        Beaumont and Fletcher.

ANNABEL LEE.

I T was many and many a year ago,
  In a kingdom by the sea,
That a maiden there lived whom you may know
  By the name of Annabel Lee ;
And this maiden she lived with no other thought
  Than to love and be loved by me.

I was a child and *she* was a child,
  In this kingdom by the sea :
But we loved with a love that was more than love—
  I and my Annabel Lee ;
With a love that the wingèd seraphs of heaven
  Coveted her and me.

And this was the reason that, long ago,
   In this kingdom by the sea,
A wind blew out of a cloud, chilling
   My beautiful Annabel Lee;
So that her high-born kinsman came
   And bore her away from me,
To shut her up in a sepulchre
   In this kingdom by the sea.

The angels, not half so happy in heaven,
   Went envying her and me—
Yes!—that was the reason (as all men know,
   In this kingdom by the sea)
That the wind came out of the cloud by night,
   Chilling and killing my Annabel Lee.

But our love it was stronger by far than the love
   Of those who were older than we—
   Of many far wiser than we—
And neither the angels in heaven above,
   Nor the demons down under the sea,
Can ever dissever my soul from the soul
   Of the beautiful Annabel Lee:

For the moon never beams, without bringing me dreams
   Of the beautiful Annabel Lee:
And the stars never rise, but I feel the bright eyes
   Of the beautiful Annabel Lee;
And so, all the night-tide, I lie down by the side
Of my darling—my darling—my life and my bride,
   In the sepulchre there by the sea,
   In her tomb by the sounding sea.

                     E. A. Poe.

SCHOOL-BOY DAYS.

ARTHUR PENDENNIS'S schoolfellows at the Greyfriars School state
that, as a boy, he was in no ways remarkable either as a dunce or
as a scholar. He never read to improve himself out of school-hours, but,
on the contrary, devoured all the novels, plays, and poetry, on which he
could lay his hands. He never was flogged, but it was a wonder how he
escaped the whipping-post. When he had money he spent it royally in
tarts for himself and his friends; he has been known to disburse nine and
sixpence out of ten shillings awarded to him in a single day. When he
had no funds he went on tick. When he could get no credit he went
without, and was almost as happy. He has been known to take a thrash-
ing for a crony without saying a word; but a blow, ever so slight, from a
friend, would make him roar. To fighting he was averse from his earliest
youth, as indeed to physic, the Greek Grammar, or any other exertion,
and would engage in none of them, except at the last extremity. He
seldom if ever told lies, and never bullied little boys. Those masters or
seniors who were kind to him, he loved with boyish ardour. And though
the Doctor, when he did not know his Horace, or could not construe his
Greek play, said that that boy Pendennis was a disgrace to the school, a
candidate for ruin in this world, and perdition in the next; a profligate
who would most likely bring his venerable father to ruin and his mother
to a dishonoured grave, and the like—yet as the Doctor made use of these
compliments to most of the boys in the place, (which has not turned out
an unusual number of felons and pickpockets,) little Pen, at first uneasy
and terrified by these charges, became gradually accustomed to hear them;
and he has not, in fact, either murdered his parents, or committed any act
worthy of transportation or hanging up to the present day.

Thackeray.

THE BEST THINGS.

WHAT wisdom more, what better life, than pleaseth God to send?
What worldly goods, what longer use, than pleaseth God to lend?
What better fare than well content, agreeing with thy wealth?
What better guest than trusty friend, in sickness and in health?
What better bed than conscience good, to pass the night with sleep?
What better work than daily care from sin thyself to keep?
What better thought than think on God, and daily Him to serve?
What better gift than to the poor, that ready be to starve?
What greater praise of God and man than mercy for to show?
Who, merciless, shall mercy find, that mercy shows to few?
What worse despair than loath to die, for fear to go to hell?
What greater faith than trust in God, through Christ in heaven to dwell?

Tusser.

NO AGE CONTENT.

LAID in my quiet bed, in study as I were,
    I saw, within my troubled head, a heap of thoughts appear;
And every thought did show so lively in mine eyes,
That now I sigh'd, and then I smiled, as cause of thoughts did rise.

I saw the little boy, and thought how oft that he
Did wish of God, to 'scape the rod, a tall young man to be;
The young man eke, that feels his bones with pains oppress'd,
How he would be a rich old man, to live and lie at rest.

The rich old man, that sees his end draw on so sore,
How he would be a man again, to live so much the more.
Whereat full oft I smiled, to see how all these three,
From boy to man, from man to boy, would chop and change degree.

Earl of Surrey.

A MODERN CRITIC.

A MODERN critic is a corrector of the press, gratis; and as he does it for nothing, so is it to no purpose. He fancies himself clerk of Stationers' Hall, and nothing must pass current that is not entered by him. He is very severe in his supposed office, and cries, "Woe to ye scribes," right or wrong. He supposes all writers to be malefactors without clergy, that claim the privilege of their books, and will not allow it, where the law of the land and common justice do. He censures in gross, and condemns all without examining particulars. If they will not confess and accuse themselves, he will rack them until they do. He is a committee man in the Commonwealth of Letters, and as great a tyrant; so is not bound to proceed but by his own rules, which he will not endure to be disputed. He has been an apocryphal scribbler himself; but his writings wanting authority he grew discontent, and turned apostate, and thence becomes so severe to those of his own profession. He never commends anything but in opposition to something else, that he would undervalue, and commonly sides with the weakest, which is generous anywhere but in judging. He is worse than an *index expurgatorius;* for he blots out all, and when he cannot find a fault, makes one. He "demurs" to all writers, and when he is "overruled," will run into "contempt." He is always bringing "writs of error," like a pettifogger, and "reversing of judgments," though the case be never so plain. He is a mountebank, that is always quacking of the infirm and diseased parts of books, to show his skill; but has nothing at all to do with the sound. He is a very ungentle reader, for he reads sentences on all authors that have the unhappiness to come before him; and therefore pedants, that stand in fear of him, always appeal from him beforehand, by the names of Momus and Zoilus, complain sorely of his extrajudicial proceedings, and protest against him as corrupt, and his judgment "void and of none effect;" and put themselves into the protection of some  powerful patron, who, like a knight-errant, is to encounter with the magician, and free them from his enchantments.

Butler.

THE SOUL'S ERRAND.

G O, Soul, the Body's guest,
  Upon a thankless errand;
Fear not to touch the best;
  The truth shall be thy warrant.
Go, since I needs must die,
And give them all the lie.

Go, tell the Court it glows,
  And shines like painted wood;
Go, tell the Church it shows
  What's good, but does no good.
If Court and Church reply,
Give Court and Church the lie.

Tell Potentates, they live
  Acting, but, oh! their actions
Not loved, unless they give;
  Nor strong, but by their factions.
If Potentates reply,
Give Potentates the lie.

Tell men of high condition,
  That rule affairs of state,
Their purpose is ambition;
  Their practice only hate.
And if they do reply,
Then give them all the lie.

Tell those that brave it most,
  They beg for more by spending,
Who, in their greatest cost,
  Seek nothing but commending.
And if they make reply,
Spare not to give the lie.

Tell Zeal it lacks devotion ;
   Tell Love it is but lust ;
Tell Time it is but motion ;
   Tell Flesh it is but dust :
And wish them not reply,
For thou must give the lie.

Tell Age it daily wasteth ;
   Tell Honour how it alters ;
Tell Beauty that it blasteth ;
   Tell Favour that she falters :
And as they do reply,
Give every one the lie.

Tell Wit how much it wrangles
   In fickle points of niceness ;
Tell Wisdom she entangles
   Herself in over-wiseness :
And if they do reply,
Then give them both the lie.

Tell Physic of her boldness ;
   Tell Skill it is pretension ;
Tell Charity of coldness ;
   Tell Law it is contention :
And if they yield reply,
Then give them still the lie.

Tell Fortune of her blindness ;
   Tell Nature of decay ;
Tell Friendship of unkindness ;
   Tell Justice of delay :
And if they do reply,
Then give them all the lie.

Tell Arts they have no soundness,
　But vary by esteeming;
Tell Schools they lack profoundness,
　And stand too much on seeming.
If Arts and Schools reply,
Give Arts and Schools the lie.

Tell Faith it's fled the city;
　Tell how the Country erreth;
Tell Manhood, shakes off pity;
　Tell Virtue, least preferreth.
And if they do reply,
Spare not to give the lie.

So, when thou hast, as I
　Commanded thee, done blabbing;
Although to give the lie
　Deserves no less than stabbing;
Yet stab at thee who will,
No stab the Soul can kill.

Sir Walter Raleigh.

GLORY AND TAXATION.

WHAT are the inevitable consequences of being too fond of glory?—Taxes upon every article which enters into the mouth, or covers the back, or is placed under the foot—taxes upon everything which it is pleasant to see, hear, feel, smell, or taste—taxes on everything on earth, and the waters under the earth—on everything that comes from abroad, or is grown at home—taxes on the raw material—taxes on every fresh value that is added to it by the industry of man—taxes on the sauce which pampers man's appetite, and the drug that restores him to health—on the ermine which decorates the judge, and the rope which hangs the criminal—on the poor man's salt and the rich man's spice—on the brass nails of the coffin, and the ribbons of the bride—at bed or board, *couchant* or *levant*, we must pay. The schoolboy whips his taxed top—the beardless youth manages his taxed horse, with a taxed bridle, on a taxed road; and the dying Englishman, pouring his medicine, which has paid seven per cent., into a spoon that has paid fifteen per cent.—flings himself back upon his chintz bed, which has paid twenty-two per cent.—and expires in the arms of an apothecary who has paid a licence of a hundred pounds for the privilege of putting him to death. His whole property is then immediately taxed from two to ten per cent. Besides the probate, large fees are demanded for burying him in the chancel; his virtues are handed down to posterity on taxed marble; and he is then gathered to his fathers—to be taxed no more. *Sydney Smith.*

PROVERBS FROM POPE.

THE proper study of mankind is man
Order is Heaven's first law.
An honest man 's the noblest work of God.
Virtue alone is happiness below.
All our knowledge is, ourselves to know.
A saint in crape is twice a saint in lawn.
Who shall decide when doctors disagree?
Gentle dulness ever loves a joke.

A SAILOR

IS a pitched piece of reason calked and tackled and only studied to dispute with tempests. He is part of his own provision for he lives ever pickled. A forewind is the substance of his creed, and fresh water the burden of his prayers. He is naturally ambitious, for he is ever climbing; out of which as naturally he fears, for he is ever flying; time and he are everywhere, ever contending who shall arrive first; he is well winded, for he tires the day, and outruns darkness. His life is like a hawk's, the best part mewed; and if he live till three coats, is a master. He sees God's wonders in the deep, but so as rather they appear his playfellows than stirrers of his zeal; nothing but hunger and hard rocks can convert him, and then but his upper deck only, for his hold neither fears nor hopes. His sleeps are but reprievals of his dangers, and when he wakes it is but next stage to dying. His wisdom is the coldest part about him, for it ever points to the north; and it lies lowest, which makes his valour every tide overflow it. In a storm it is disputable whether the noise be more his or the elements, and which will first leave scolding; on which side of the ship he may be saved best, whether his faith be starboard faith or larboard; or the helm at that time not all his hope of heaven; his keel is the emblem of his conscience, till it be split he never repents, then no further than the land allows him, and his language is a new confusion, and all his thoughts new nations; his body and his ship are both one burden, nor is it known which stows most wine or rolls most, only the ship is guided, he has no stern; a barnacle and he are bred together, both of one nature, and it is feared one reason; upon any but a wooden horse he cannot ride, and if the wind blow against him he dare not; he swarves up to his seat as to a sailyard, and cannot sit unless he bear a flagstaff; if ever he be broken to the saddle it is but a voyage still, for he mistakes the bridle for a bowline, and is ever turning his horse's tail; he can pray, but it is by rote, not faith, and when he would he dares not, for his brackish belief hath made that ominous. A rock or a quicksand plucks him before he be ripe, else he is gathered to his friends at Wapping.

Sir Thomas Overbury.

BOBADIL'S MODE OF WARFARE.

I WILL tell you, by the way of private, and under seal, I am a gentleman, and live here obscure, and to myself: but were I known to his majesty, and the lords, observe me, I would undertake, upon this poor head and life, for the public benefit of the state, not only to spare the entire lives of his subjects in general, but to save the one half, nay, three parts of his yearly charge in holding war, and against what enemy soever. And how would I do it, think you? Why, thus :—I would select nineteen more to myself; gentlemen they should be, of a good spirit, strong, and able constitution; I would choose them by an instinct, a character that I have; and I would teach these nineteen the special rules; as your Punto, your Reverso, your Stoccata, your Imbrocata, your Passada, your Montonto; till they could all play very nearly, or altogether, as well as myself. This done, say the enemy were forty thousand strong; we twenty would come into the field the tenth of March, or thereabouts; and we would challenge twenty of the enemy; they could not, in their honour, refuse us! Well, we would kill them;—challenge twenty more, kill them;—twenty more, kill them;—twenty more, kill them too;—and thus would we kill every man his twenty a-day! That's twenty score;—twenty score, that's two hundred;—two hundred a-day, five days a thousand :—forty thousand, forty times five, five times forty, . . . two hundred days kills them all up, by computation! And this I will venture my poor gentlemanlike carcass to perform—provided there be no treason practised upon us—by fair and discreet manhood; that is, civilly by the sword.   *Ben Jonson.*

THOUGHTS ON VARIOUS SUBJECTS.

WHEN a true genius appeareth in the world, you may know him by this infallible sign, that the dunces are all in confederacy against him.

It is in disputes as in armies, where the weaker side setteth up false lights, and maketh a great noise, that the enemy may believe them to be more numerous and strong than they really are.

I have known some men possessed of good qualities, which were very serviceable to others, but useless to themselves; like a sun-dial on the front of a house, to inform the neighbours and passengers, but not the owner within.

The power of fortune is confessed only by the miserable, for the happy impute all their success to prudence and merit.

Ambition often puts men upon doing the meanest offices; so, climbing is performed in the same posture with creeping.

Censure is the tax a man payeth to the public for being eminent.

No wise man ever wished to be younger.

An idle reason lessens the weight of the good ones you gave before.

Complaint is the largest tribute Heaven receives, and the sincerest part of our devotion.

To be vain is rather a mark of humility than pride. Vain men delight in telling what honours have been done them, what great company they have kept, and the like; by which they plainly confess that these honours were more than their due, and such as their friends would not believe if they had not been told: whereas a man truly proud thinks the greatest honours below his merit, and consequently scorns to boast. I therefore deliver it as a maxim, that whoever desires the character of a proud man, ought to conceal his vanity.

Whoever can make two ears of corn or two blades of grass grow where only one grew before, will deserve better of mankind, and do more essential service to his country than the whole race of politicians put together.

False happiness is like false money, it passes for a time as well as the true, and serves ordinary occasions; but when it is brought to the touch, we find the lightness and alloy, and feel the loss.

Dean Swift.

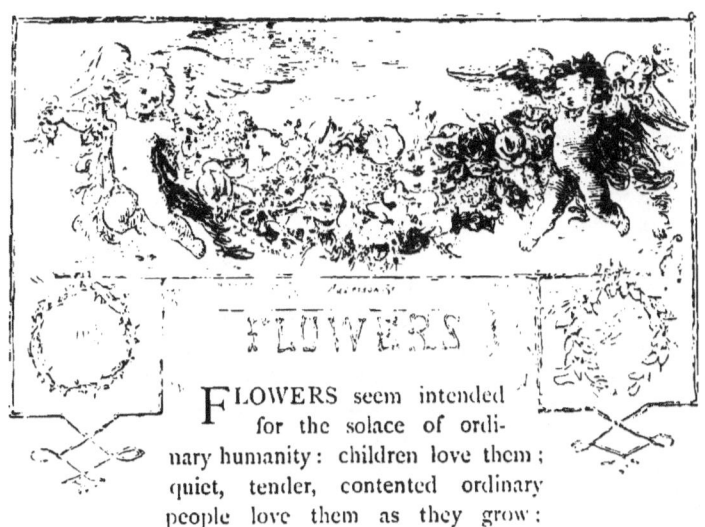

FLOWERS seem intended for the solace of ordinary humanity: children love them; quiet, tender, contented ordinary people love them as they grow: luxurious and disorderly people rejoice in them gathered. They are the cottager's treasure; and in the crowded town, mark, as with a little broken fragment of rainbow, the windows of the workers in whose heart rests the covenant of peace. Passionate or religious minds contemplate them with fond, feverish intensity; the affection is seen severely calm in the works of many old religious painters, and mixed with more open and true country sentiment in those of our own pre-Raphaelites. To the child and the girl, the peasant and the manufacturing operative, to the grisette and the nun, the lover and the monk, they are precious always. But to the men of supreme power and thoughtfulness, precious only at times; symbolically and pathetically often to the poets, but rarely for their own sake. They fall forgotten from the great workman's and soldier's hands. Such men will take, in thankfulness, crowns of leaves, or crowns of thorns —not crowns of flowers.

Ruskin.

A TOUCH OF CONSCIENCE.

I REMEMBER a touch of conscience at school. My good old aunt, who never parted from me at the end of a holiday without stuffing a sweet-meat, or some nice thing, into my pocket, had dismissed me one evening with a smoking plum-cake, fresh from the oven. In my way to school (it was over London Bridge) a gray-headed old beggar saluted me, (I have no doubt at this time of day that he was a counterfeit.) I had no pence to console him with, and in the vanity of self-denial, and in the very coxcombry of charity, school-boy-like, I made him a present of—the whole cake! I walked on a little, buoyed up, as one is on such occasions, with a sweet soothing of self-satisfaction; but before I had got to the end of the bridge, my better feelings returned, and I burst into tears, thinking how ungrateful I had been to my good aunt, to go and give her good gift away to a stranger, that I had never seen before, and who might be a bad man for aught I knew; and then I thought of the pleasure my aunt would be taking in thinking that I—I myself, and not another—would eat her nice cake—and what should I say to her the next time I saw her—how naughty I was to part with her pretty present—and the odour of that spicy cake came back upon my recollection, and the pleasure and the curiosity I had taken in seeing her make it, and her joy when she sent it to the oven, and how disappointed she would feel that I had never had a bit of it in my mouth at last—and I blamed my impertinent spirit of alms giving, and out-of-place hypocrisy of goodness, and above all I wished never to see the face again of that insidious, good-for-nothing, old gray impostor.

              Charles Lamb.

A MILK AND WATER EPIGRAM.

"ARE good folk very clean up town?"
  Inquired a rustic o'er his porter.
"Clean!" cried a cockney just come down,
  "They even wash their milk with water."

COUPLETS FROM POPE.

'TIS with our judgments as our watches; none
Go just alike, yet each believes his own.

A little learning is a dangerous thing!
Drink deep, or taste not the Pierian spring.

True wit is nature to advantage dress'd,
What oft was thought, but ne'er so well express'd.

Words are like leaves; and where they most abound,
Much fruit of sense beneath is rarely found.

Envy will merit, as its shade, pursue;
But, like a shadow, prove the substance true.

Good nature and good sense must ever join;
To err is human, to forgive, divine.

Hope springs eternal in the human breast:
Man never is, but always to be blest.

Vice is a monster of so frightful mien,
As, to be hated, needs but to be seen.

Honour and state from no condition rise;
Act well your part, there all the honour lies.

'Tis education forms the common mind,
And as the twig is bent, the tree's inclined.

Good sense, which only is the gift of Heaven,
And, though no science, fairly worth the seven.

SERMONS IN STONES.

THERE are no natural objects out of which more can be thus learned
than out of stones. They seem to have been created especially to
reward a patient observer. Nearly all other objects in nature can be seen,
to some extent, without patience, and are pleasant even in being half seen.
Trees, clouds, and rivers are enjoyable even by the careless; but the stone
under his foot has for carelessness nothing in it but stumbling: no pleasure is languidly to be had out of it, nor food, nor good of any kind;
nothing but symbolism of the hard heart and the unfatherly gift. And
yet, do but give it some reverence and watchfulness, and there is bread
of thought in it, more than in any other lowly feature of all the landscape.
For a stone, when it is examined, will be found a mountain in miniature.
The fineness of Nature's work is so great, that, into a single block, a foot
or two in diameter, she can compress as many changes of form and struc-
ture, in a small scale, as she needs for her mountains on a large one; and
taking moss for forests, and grains of crystal for crags, the surface of a
stone, in by far the plurality of instances, is more interesting than the
surface of an ordinary hill; more fantastic in form, and incomparably
richer in colour.

Ruskin.

LOVE IN MAN AND WOMAN.

IT is an old and received truism—love is an hour with us: it is all night
and all day with a woman. Damon has taxes, sermon, parade, tailors'
bills, parliamentary duties, and the deuce knows what to think of; Delia
has to think about Damon—Damon is the oak, (or the post,) and stands
up, and Delia is the ivy or the honeysuckle whose arms twine about him.
Is it not so, Delia? Is it not your nature to creep about his feet and kiss
them, to twine round his trunk and hang there; and Damon's to stand
like a British man with his hands in his breeches pocket, while the pretty
fond parasite clings round him?

Thackeray.

THE SORROWS OF WERTER.

WERTER had a love for Charlotte,
  Such as words could never utter;
Would you know how first he met her?
  She was cutting bread and butter.
So he sigh'd, and pined, and ogled,
  And his passion boiled and bubbled,
Till he blew his silly brains out,
  And no more was by it troubled.
Charlotte, having seen his body
  Borne before her on a shutter,
Like a well-conducted person,
  Went on cutting bread and butter.

Thackeray.

THE SEA.

TELL me, ye naturalists, who sounded the first march and retreat to the tide, " Hither shalt thou come, and no farther?" Why doth not the water recover his right over the earth, being higher in nature? Whence came the salt, and who first boiled it, which made so much brine? When the winds are not only wild in a storm, but even stark mad in a hurricane, who is it that restores them again to their wits, and brings them asleep in a calm? Who made the mighty whales, which swim in a sea of water. and have a sea of oil swimming in them? Who first taught the water to imitate the creatures on land, so that the sea is the stable of horse-fishes, the stall of kine-fishes, the sty of hog-fishes, the kennel of dog-fishes, and in all things the sea the ape of the land? Whence grows the ambergris in the sea? which is not so hard to find where it is as to know what it is. Was not God the first shipwright? and have not all vessels on the water descended from the loins (or ribs rather) of Noah's ark? or else, who durst be so bold, with a few crooked boards nailed together, a stick standing upright, and a rag tied to it. to adventure into the ocean? What loadstone first touched the loadstone? or how first fell it in love with the North. rather affecting that cold climate than the pleasant East, or fruitful South or West? How comes that stone to know more than men, and find the way to the land in a mist? In most of these, men take sanctuary at *occulta qualitas,* (some hidden quality,) and complain that the room is dark, when their eyes are blind. Indeed, they are God's wonders? and that seaman the greatest wonder of all for his blockishness, who, seeing them daily, neither takes notice of them, admires them, nor is thankful for them. *Fuller.*

A CLUSTER OF ARABIC PROVERBS.

A THOUSAND cranes in the air are not worth one sparrow in the fist. There are no fans in hell.
The man who makes chaff of himself will be eaten by cows.
If I were to trade in winding-sheets, my luck would make all men live.

THE WAR HORSE.

HAST thou given the horse strength? hast thou clothed his neck with thunder?

Canst thou make him afraid as a grasshopper? the glory of his nostrils is terrible.

He paweth in the valley, and rejoiceth in his strength : he goeth on to meet the armed men.

He mocketh at fear, and is not affrighted : neither turneth he back from the sword.

The quiver rattleth against him, the glittering spear and the shield.

He swalloweth the ground with fierceness and rage : neither believeth he that it is the sound of the trumpet.

He saith among the trumpets, Ha, ha ; and he smelleth the battle afar off, the thunder of the captains, and the shouting.

Book of Job.

THE BOOK OF JOB.

I CALL that, apart from all theories about it, one of the grandest things ever written with pen. One feels, indeed, as if it were not Hebrew; such a noble universality, different from noble patriotism or sectarianism, reigns in it. A noble Book; all men's Book. It is our first, oldest statement of the never-ending Problem,—man's destiny and God's ways with him here in this earth. And all in such free-flowing outlines; grand in its sincerity, in its simplicity ; in its epic melody, and repose of reconcilement. There is the seeing eye, the mildly understanding heart. So *true* every way ; true eyesight and vision for all things ; material things no less than spiritual : the Horse,—" Hast thou clothed his neck with *thunder?*" —he " *laughs* at the shaking of the spear !" Such living likenesses were never since drawn. Sublime sorrow, sublime reconciliation ; oldest choral melody as of the heart of mankind ;—so soft, and great : as the summer midnight, as the world with its seas and stars ! There is nothing written, I think, in the Bible or out of it, of equal literary merit.

Carlyle.

SUMMER.

I 'M coming along with a bounding pace,
   To finish the work that spring begun ;
I 've left them all with a brighter face,
   The flowers in the vales through which I 've run.

I have hung festoons from laburnum-trees,
   And clothed the lilac, the birch, and broom ;
I 've waken'd the sound of humming bees,
   And deck'd all nature in brighter bloom.

I 've roused the laugh of the playful child,
   And tired it out in the sunny noon ;
All nature at my approach hath smiled,
   And I 've made fond lovers seek the moon.

For this is my life, my glorious reign,
   And I 'll queen it well in my leafy bower ;
All shall be bright in my rich domain ;
   I 'm queen of the leaf, the bud, and the flower.

And I 'll reign in triumph till autumn time
   Shall conquer my green and verdant pride :
Then I 'll hie me to another clime,
   Till I 'm call'd again as a sunny bride.

THE POWER OF LITTLE THINGS.

WHEN Franklin made his discovery of the identity of lightning and electricity, it was sneered at, and people asked, "Of what use is it?" To which his apt reply was, "What is the use of a child? It may become a man!" When Galvani discovered that a frog's leg twitched when placed in contact with different metals, it could scarcely have been imagined that so apparently insignificant a fact could have led to important results. Yet therein lay the germ of the Electric Telegraph, which binds the intelligence of continents together, and probably, before many years elapse, will "put a girdle round the globe." So too, little bits of stone and fossil, dug out of the earth, intelligently interpreted, have issued in the science of geology and the practical operations of mining, in which large capitals are invested, and vast numbers of persons profitably employed.

The gigantic machinery employed in pumping our mines, working our mills and manufactories, and driving our steam-ships and locomotives, in like manner depends for its supply of power upon so slight an agency as particles of water expanded by heat. The steam which we see issuing from the common tea-kettle, when pent up within an ingeniously-contrived mechanism, displays a force equal to that of millions of horses, and contains a power to rebuke the waves, and to set even the hurricane at defiance. Nay, it is the same power at work within the bowels of the earth which has been the cause of many of those semi-miraculous catastrophes, —volcanoes and earthquakes,—that have played so mighty a part in the history of the globe. *Smiles.*

THE WORLD'S WEALTH.

THIS world's wealth, which men so much desire,
    May well be liken'd to a burning fire:
Whereof a little can do little harm,
But profit much, our bodies well to warm.
But take too much, and surely thou shalt burn;
So too much wealth to too much woe doth turn.

A PROFESSOR OF PUFFING.

I AM, sir, a practitioner in panegyric, or, to speak more plainly, a professor of the art of puffing, at your service. . . . . I daresay, now, you conceive half the very civil paragraphs and advertisements you see to be written by the parties concerned, or their friends? No such thing: nine out of ten are manufactured by me in the way of business.

Even the auctioneers now—the auctioneers, I say—though the rogues have lately got some credit for their language—not an article of the merit theirs: take them out of their pulpits, and they are as dull as catalogues! —No, sir; 'twas I enriched their style—'twas I first taught them to crowd their advertisements with panegyrical superlatives, each epithet rising above the other, like the bidders in their own auction-rooms! From me they learned to inlay their phraseology with variegated chips of exotic metaphor: by me, too, their inventive faculties were called forth:—by me they were instructed to clothe ideal walls with gratuitous fruits—to insinuate obsequious rivulets into visionary groves—to teach courteous shrubs to nod their approbation of the grateful soil: or on emergencies to raise upstart oaks, where there never had been an acorn; to create a delightful vicinage without the assistance of a neighbour; or fix the temple of Hygeia in the fens of Lincolnshire!

Sheridan.

THE SAGE'S WIT.

AS lately a sage on fine ham was repasting,
   (Though for breakfast too savoury, I ween,)
He exclaim'd to a friend, who sat silent and fasting,
   " What a breakfast of learning is mine ! "
" A breakfast of learning ! " with wonder he cried,
   And laugh'd, for he thought him mistaken ;
" Why, what is it else ? " the sage quickly replied,
   " When I'm making large extracts from Bacon ? "

OUR LITTLE REPUBLIC.

THE little republic, to which I gave laws, was regulated in the following manner: by sunrise we all assembled in our common apartment,
the fire being previously kindled by the servant. After we had saluted
each other with proper ceremony, for I always thought fit to keep up some
mechanical forms of good breeding, without which freedom ever destroys
friendship, we all bent in gratitude to that Being who gave us another
day. This duty being performed, my son and I went to pursue our usual
industry abroad, while my wife and daughters employed themselves in
providing breakfast. which was always ready at a certain time. I allowed
half-an-hour for this meal, and an hour for dinner; which time was taken
up in innocent mirth between my wife and daughters, and in philosophical
arguments between my son and me.

G

As we rose with the sun, so we never pursued our labours after it was gone down, but returned home to the expecting family, where smiling looks, a neat hearth, and pleasant fire were prepared for our reception. Nor were we without guests; sometimes Farmer Flamborough, our talkative neighbour, and often the blind piper would pay us a visit, and taste our gooseberry-wine; for the making of which we had lost neither the recipe nor the reputation. These harmless people had several ways of being good company; for, while one played, the other would sing some soothing ballad—*Johnny Armstrong's Last Go d-night*, or *The Cruelty of Barbara Allan*. The night was concluded in the manner we began the morning; my youngest boys being appointed to read the lessons of the day; and he that read loudest, distinctest, and best, was to have a half-penny on Sunday to put into the poor's-box.

Goldsmith.

A CLUSTER OF FRENCH PROVERBS.

THE fox says of the mulberries when he cannot get at them, "They are not good."

Loaves put awry into the oven come out crooked.

He pulls at a long rope who desires another's death.

The friendship of the great is like the shadow of a bush, soon gone.

Money borrowed is soon sorrowed.

With the help of an "If" you might put Paris in a bottle.

For over-buying there's no help but selling again.

He has a good pledge of the cat who has her skin.

It is nothing at all: only a woman drowning.

A hundred years is not much, but never is a long while.

He knocks boldly at the door who brings good news.

Never sell the bear skin till you have killed the bear.

The beadle of the parish is always of the vicar's opinion.

Horses run for benefices, but asses get them.

One "take this" is better than two "you shall have."

Word by word big books are made.

GENEVIEVE.

MAID of my love, sweet Genevieve !
   In Beauty's light you glide along :
Your eye is like the star of eve,
And sweet your voice as seraph's song.
Yet not your heavenly beauty gives
This heart with passion soft to glow;
Within your soul a voice there lives—
It bids you hear the tale of woe.
When sinking low the sufferer wan
Beholds no hand outstretcht to save,
Fair as the bosom of the swan
That rises graceful o'er the wave,
I've seen your breast with pity heave,
And therefore love I you, sweet Genevieve !

Coleridge.

A CLUSTER OF ITALIAN PROVERBS.

FOR the buyer a hundred eyes are too few: for the seller one is enough.
   He dances well to whom Fortune pipes.
He who errs in the tens errs in the thousands.
There is no making pancakes without breaking eggs.
He who pays before hand is served behind hand.
He who would be long an old man must begin betimes.
Credit is dead.   Bad pay killed it.
When the will is prompt the legs are nimble.
One eye of the master sees more than four eyes of his servants.
To protest and knock one's head against the wall is what everybody
   can do.
The virtue of silence is a great piece of knowledge.
If the young man knew, if the old man could, there is nothing but would
   be done.

PRAYER

PRAYER is the soul's sincere desire,
    Utter'd or unexpress'd;
The motion of a hidden fire
    That trembles in the breast.

Prayer is the burden of a sigh,
    The falling of a tear;
The upward glancing of an eye,
    When none but God is near.

Prayer is the simplest form of speech
    That infant lips can try;
Prayer, the sublimest strains that reach
    The Majesty on high.

Prayer is the Christian's vital breath,
    The Christian's native air;
His watchward at the gates of death—
    He enters heaven by prayer.

Prayer is the contrite sinner's voice,
    Returning from his ways;
While angels in their songs rejoice,
    And cry, " Behold, he prays! "

The saints in prayer appear as one,
    In word, and deed, and mind;
While with the Father and the Son,
    Sweet fellowship they find.

Here on the hills He feeds His herds,
    His flocks on yonder plains;
His praise is warbled by the birds;
    Oh, could we catch their strains!

O Thou ! by whom we come to God,
The Life, the Truth, the Way;
The path of prayer Thyself hast trod;
Lord, teach us how to pray.

As fail the waters from the deep,
As summer brooks run dry,
Man lieth down in dreamless sleep,
His life is vanity.

Man lieth down, no more to wake,
Till yonder arching sphere
Shall with a roll of thunder break,
And nature disappear.

Oh ! hide me till Thy wrath be past,
Thou, who canst slay or save !
Hide me where hope may anchor fast,
In my Redeemer's grave !

James Montgomery.

MAN.

M EN are but children of a larger growth,
Our appetites as apt to change as theirs,
And full as craving too, and full as vain ;
And yet the soul, shut up in her dark room,
Viewing so clear abroad, at home sees nothing ;
But, like a mole in earth, busy and blind,
Works all her folly up, and casts it outward
To the world's open view. *Dryden.*

JOHN BULL

THERE is no species of humour in which the English more excel than that which consists in caricaturing and giving ludicrous appellations or nicknames. In this way they have whimsically designated, not merely individuals, but nations; and, in their fondness for pushing a joke, they have not spared even themselves. One would think that, in personifying itself, a nation would be apt to picture something grand, heroic, and imposing; but it is characteristic of the peculiar humour of the English, and of their love for what is blunt, comic, and familiar, that they have embodied their national oddities in the figure of a sturdy, corpulent old fellow, with a three-cornered hat, red waistcoat, leather breeches, and stout oaken cudgel. Thus they have taken a singular delight in exhibiting their most private foibles in a laughable point of view; and have been so successful in their delineations, that there is scarcely a being in actual existence more absolutely present to the public mind than that eccentric personage, John Bull.

John Bull, to all appearance, is a plain,

downright, matter-of-fact fellow, with much less of poetry about him than rich prose. There is little of romance in his nature, but a vast deal of strong natural feeling. He excels in humour more than in wit; is jolly rather than gay; melancholy rather than morose; can easily be moved to a sudden tear, or surprised into a broad laugh; but he loathes sentiment, and has no turn for light pleasantry. He is a boon companion, if you allow him to have his humour, and to talk about himself; and he will stand by a friend in a quarrel, with life and purse, however soundly he may be cudgelled.

In this last respect, to tell the truth, he has a propensity to be somewhat too ready. He is a busy-minded personage, who thinks not merely for himself and family, but for all the country round, and is most generously disposed to be everybody's champion. He is continually volunteering his services to settle his neighbour's affairs, and takes it in great dudgeon if they engage in any matter of consequence without asking his advice; though he seldom engages in any friendly office of the kind without finishing by getting into a squabble with all parties, and then railing bitterly at their ingratitude. He unluckily took lessons in his youth in the noble science of defence, and having accomplished himself

in the use of his limbs and his weapons, and become a perfect master at boxing and cudgel play, he has had a troublesome life of it ever since. He cannot hear of a quarrel between the most distant of his neighbours but he begins incontinently to fumble with the head of his cudgel, and consider whether his interest or honour does not require that he should meddle in the broil.

He is a little fond of playing the magnifico abroad : of pulling out a long purse; flinging his money bravely about at boxing-matches, horse-races, cock-fights, and carrying a high head among " gentlemen of the fancy ;" but immediately after one of these fits of extravagance, he will be taken with violent qualms of economy; stop short at the most trivial expenditure ; talk desperately of being ruined and brought upon the parish ; and in such moods will not pay the smallest tradesman's bill without violent altercation. He is, in fact, the most punctual and discontented paymaster in the world ; drawing his coin out of his breeches-pocket with infinite reluctance ; paying to the uttermost farthing, but accompanying every guinea with a growl.

Washington Irving.

A CONTENTED MIND.

WHEN all is done and said,
In the end thus shall you find,
He most of all doth bathe in bliss
That hath a quiet mind.

Companion none is like
Unto the mind alone,
For many have been harm'd by speech—
Through thinking few or none.

Our wealth leaves us at death,
Our kinsmen at the grave;
But virtue of the mind unto
The heavens with us we have.

Wherefore for virtue's sake
I can be well content,
The sweetest time of all my life
To deem in thinking spent.

Earl of Surrey.

A CLUSTER OF TURKISH PROVERBS.

" IT is a fast-day to-day, and I must not eat," says the cat, when she
cannot reach the liver.
Honey is a good thing, but the price of honey is another thing.
Death is a black camel that kneels once before every door.
Fame is not gained on a feather bed.
Which are the most beautiful birds? "My little ones," said the crow.
The lazy man says, " I have no strength."

LOVE.

ALL thoughts, all passions, all delights,
  Whatever stirs this mortal frame,
All are but ministers of Love,
    And feed his sacred flame.

Oft in my waking dreams do I
Live o'er again that happy hour,
When midway on the mount I lay
    Beside the ruin'd tower.

The moonshine stealing o'er the scene
Had blended with the lights of eve ;
And she was there, my hope, my joy,
    My own dear Genevieve !

She lean'd against the arméd man,
The statue of the arméd knight ;
She stood and listen'd to my lay,
    Amid the lingering light.

Few sorrows hath she of her own
My hope ! my joy ! my Genevieve !
She loves me best, whene'er I sing
    The songs that make her grieve.

I play'd a soft and doleful air,
I sang an old and moving story—
An old rude song, that suited well.
    That ruin wild and hoary.

She listen'd with a flitting blush,
With downcast eyes and modest grace ;
For well she knew, I could not choose
    But gaze upon her face.

I told her of the Knight that wore
Upon his shield a burning brand ;
And that for ten long years he woo'd
    The Lady of the Land.

I told her how he pined : and ah !
The deep, the low, the pleading tone
With which I sang another's love
    Interpreted my own.

She listen'd with a flitting blush,
With downcast eyes, and modest grace ;
And she forgave me, that I gazed
    Too fondly on her face.

But when I told the cruel scorn
That crazed that bold and lovely Knight,
And that he cross'd the mountain-woods,
    Nor rested day nor night ;

That sometimes from the savage den,
And sometimes from the darksome shade,
And sometimes starting up at once
    In green and sunny glade

There came and look'd him in the face
An angel beautiful and bright ;
And that he knew it was a Fiend,
    This miserable Knight !

And that unknowing what he did,
He leap'd amid a murderous band,
And saved from outrage worse than death
    The Lady of the Land;

And how she wept, and clasp'd his knees,
And how she tended him in vain;
And ever strove to expiate
    The scorn that crazed his brain;

And that she nursed him in a cave,
And how his madness went away,
When on the yellow forest-leaves
    A dying man he lay;

—His dying words—but when I reach'd
That tenderest strain of all the ditty,
My faltering voice and pausing harp
    Disturb'd her soul with pity!

All impulses of soul and sense
Had thrill'd my guileless Genevieve;
The music and the doleful tale,
    The rich and balmy eve:

And hopes, and fears that kindle hope,
An undistinguishable throng,
And gentle wishes long subdued,
    Subdued and cherish'd long!

She wept with pity and delight,
She blush'd with love and virgin shame;
And like the murmur of a dream,
    I heard her breathe my name.

Her bosom heaved—she stepp'd aside,
As conscious of my look she stept—
Then suddenly, with timorous eye
 She fled to me and wept.

She half enclosed me with her arms,
She press'd me with a meek embrace;
And bending back her head, look'd up,
 And gazed upon my face.

'Twas partly love, and partly fear,
And partly 'twas a bashful art,
That I might rather feel than see
 The swelling of her heart.

I calm'd her fears, and she was calm,
And told her love with virgin pride;
And so I won my Genevieve,
 My bright and beauteous bride.

S. T. Coleridge.

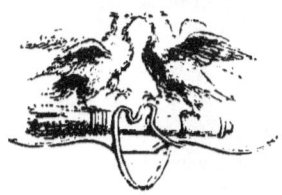

BEAUTY.

VIRTUE is like a rich stone, best plain set; and surely virtue is best in a body that is comely, though not of delicate features; and that hath rather dignity of presence than beauty of aspect; neither is it almost seen, that very beautiful persons are otherwise of great virtue; as if nature were rather busy not to err, than in labour to produce excellency; and therefore they prove accomplished, but not of great spirit; and study rather behaviour, than virtue. But this holds not always; for Augustus Cæsar, Titus Vespasianus, Philip le Bel of France, Edward the Fourth of England, Alcibiades of Athens, Ismael, the sofi of Persia, were all high and great spirits, and yet the most beautiful men of their times. In beauty, that of favour, is more than that of colour; and that of decent and gracious motion, more than that of favour. That is the best part of beauty which a picture cannot express; no, nor the first sight of the life. There is no excellent beauty that hath not some strangeness in the proportion. A man cannot tell whether Apelles or Albert Durer were the more trifler; whereof the one would make a personage by geometrical proportions; the other, by taking the best parts out of divers faces to make one excellent. Such personages, I think, would please nobody but the painter that made them; not but I think a painter may make a better face than ever was; but he must do it by a kind of felicity, (as a musician that maketh an excellent air in music,) and not by rule. A man shall see faces, that if you examine them part by part, you shall find never a good; and yet altogether do well. If it be true that the principal part of beauty is in decent motion, certainly it is no marvel, though persons in years seem many times more amiable; *pulchrorum autumnus pulcher;* for no youth can be comely but by pardon, and considering the youth as to make up the comeliness. Beauty is as summer fruits, which are easy to corrupt and cannot last; and, for the most part, it makes a dissolute youth, and an age a little out of countenance; but yet certainly again, if it light well, it maketh virtues shine, and vices blush.

Bacon.

THE RAM AND ITS SHADOW.

ON the green turf, with his imperial front
    Shaggy and bold, and wreathèd horns superb,
The breathing creature stood : as beautiful
Beneath him, show'd his shadowy counterpart.
Each had his glowing mountains, each his sky,
And each seem'd centre of his own fair world :
Antipodes unconscious of each other,
Yet, in partition, with their several spheres,
Blended in perfect stillness, to our sight!   *Wordsworth*

I

WHAT IS POETRY?

IF a young reader should ask, after all, What is the best way of knowing
bad poets from good, the best poets from the next best, and so on?
the answer is, the only and twofold way; first, the perusal of the best
poets with the greatest attention; and second, the cultivation of that love
of truth and beauty which made them what they are. Every true reader
of poetry partakes of a more than ordinary portion of the poetic nature;
and no one can be completely such, who does not love, or take an
interest in everything that interests the poet, from the firmament to the
daisy — from the highest heart of man to the most pitiable of the low.
It is a good practice to read with pen in hand, marking what is liked or
doubted. It rivets the attention, realises the greatest amount of enjoyment, and facilitates reference. It enables the reader also, from time to
time, to see what progress he makes with his own mind, and how it grows
up to the stature of its exalter.

If the same person should ask, What class of poetry is the highest? I
should say, undoubtedly, the Epic: for it includes the drama, with narra-
tion besides; or the speaking and action of the characters, with the speaking of the poet himself, whose utmost address is taxed to relate all well
for so long a time, particularly in the passages least sustained by enthu-
siasm. Whether this class has included the greatest poet, is another
question still under trial; for Shakespeare perplexes all such verdicts,
even when the claimant is Homer; though if a judgment may be drawn
from his early narratives, (" Venus and Adonis," and the " Rape of
Lucrece,") it is to be doubted whether even Shakespeare could have told
a story like Homer, owing to that incessant activity and superfœtation of
thought, a little less of which might be occasionally desired even in his
plays;—if it were possible, once possessing anything of his, to wish it
away. Next to Homer and Shakespeare come such narrators as the less
universal but intenser Dante; Milton, with his dignified imagination; the
universal profoundly simple Chaucer; and luxuriant remote Spenser—
immortal child in poetry's most poetic solitudes: then the great second-
rate dramatists: unless those who are better acquainted with Greek
tragedy than I am, demand a place for them before Chaucer: then the

airy yet robust universality of Ariosto; the hearty out-of-door nature of
Theocritus, also a universalist; the finest lyrical poets, (who only take
short flights, compared with the narrators;) the purely contemplative
poets, who have more thought than feeling; the descriptive, satirical,
didactic, epigrammatic. It is to be borne in mind, however, that the
first poet of an inferior class may be superior to followers in the train of
a higher one, though the superiority is by no means to be taken for
granted; otherwise Pope would be superior to Fletcher, and Butler to
Pope. Imagination, teeming with action and character, makes the
greatest poets; feeling and thought the next; fancy (by itself) the next;
wit the last.

What the poet has to cultivate above all things is love and truth;—
what he has to avoid, like poison, is the fleeting and the false. He will
get no good by proposing to be "in earnest at the moment." His
earnestness must be innate and habitual; born with him, and felt to be
his most precious inheritance. "I expect neither profit nor general fame
by my writings," says Coleridge, in the Preface to his Poems; "and I
consider myself as having been amply repaid without either. Poetry has
been to me its *own exceeding great reward:* it has soothed my afflictions;
it has multiplied and refined my enjoyments; it has endeared solitude;
and it has given me the habit of wishing to discover the good and the
beautiful in all that meets and surrounds me."

"Poetry," says Shelley, "lifts the veil from the hidden beauty of the
world, *and makes familiar objects be as if they were not familiar.* It repro-
duces all that it represents; and the impersonations clothed in its Elysian
light stand thenceforward in the minds of those who have once contem-
plated them, as memorials of that gentle and exalted content which extends itself over all thoughts and actions with which it coexists. The
great secret of morals is love, or of going out of our own nature, and an
identification of ourselves with the beautiful which exists in thought,
action, or person, not our own. A man, to be greatly good, must imagine
intensely and comprehensively; he must put himself in the place of
another, and of many others; the pains and pleasures of his species must
become his own. The great instrument of moral good is imagination:
and poetry administers to the effect by acting upon the cause."

Leigh Hunt.

SCOTLAND
IN 1798

IT requires a surgical operation to get a joke well into a Scotch understanding. Their only idea of wit, or rather that inferior variety of this electric talent which prevails occasionally in the North, and which under the name of wut, is so indefinitely distressing to people of good taste, is laughing immoderately at stated intervals. They are so imbued with metaphysics that they even make love metaphysically. I overheard a young lady of my acquaintance, at a dance in Edinburgh, exclaim, in a sudden pause of the music, " What you say, my lord, is very true of love in the *aibstract*, but—" here the fiddlers began fiddling furiously, and the rest was lost. No nation has so large a stock of benevolence of heart. If you meet with an accident, half Edinburgh immediately flocks to your door to inquire after your *puir* hand or your *puir* foot, and with a degree of interest that convinces you their whole hearts are in the inquiry. You find they usually arrange their dishes at dinner by the points of the compass—" Sandy, put the gigot of mutton to the south, and move the singet sheep's-head a wee bit to the nor-wast." If you knock at the door, you hear a shrill female voice from the fifth flat shriek out, " Wha 's chapping at' the door?" which is presently opened by a lassie with short petticoats, bare legs, and thick ankles. My Scotch servants bargained they were not to have salmon more than three times a-week, and always pulled off their stockings, in spite of my repeated objurgations, the moment my back was turned. Their temper stands anything but an attack on their climate. They would have you even believe they can ripen fruit; and to be candid, I must own in remarkably warm summers I have tasted peaches that made most excellent pickles; and it is upon record that at the siege of Perth, on one occasion, the ammunition failing, their nectarines made admirable cannon-balls. Even the enlightened mind of Jeffrey cannot shake off the illusion that myrtles flourished at Craig Crook. In vain I have represented to him that they are of the genus *Carduus*, and pointed out their prickly peculiarities. In vain I have reminded him that I have seen hackney coaches drawn by four horses in the winter on account of the snow; that I had rescued a man blown flat against my door by the violence of the winds, and black in the face; that even the experienced Scotch fowls did not venture to cross the streets, but sidled along, tails aloft, without venturing to encounter the gale. Jeffrey sticks to his myrtle illusions, and treats my attacks with as much contempt as if I had been a wild visionary, who had never breathed his caller air, nor lived and suffered under the rigour of his climate, nor spent five years in discussing metaphysics and medicine in that garret of the earth—that knuckle-end of England—that land of Calvin, oat-cakes, and sulphur.

Sydney Smith.

A WILD NIGHT AT SEA.

ON, on, on, over the countless miles of angry space, roll the long heaving billows. Mountains and caves are here, and yet are not; for what is now the one, is now the other: then all is but a boiling heap of rushing water. Pursuit, and flight, and mad return of wave on wave, and savage struggling, ending in a spouting up of foam that whitens the black night; incessant change of place, and form, and hue; constancy in nothing but eternal strife; on, on, on they roll, and darker grows the night, and louder howl the winds, and more clamorous and fierce become the million voices in the sea—when the wild cry goes forth upon the storm, " A ship!"

Onward she comes, in gallant combat with the elements, her tall masts trembling, and her timbers starting on the strain; onward she comes, now high upon the curling billows, now low down in the hollows of the sea, as hiding for the moment from its fury: and every storm-voice in the air and water cries more loudly yet, " A ship!"

Still she comes striving on: and at her boldness and the spreading cry, the angry waves rise up above each other's hoary heads to look; and round about the vessel, far as the mariners on her decks can pierce into the gloom, they press upon her, forcing each other down, and starting up and rushing forward from afar, in dreadful curiosity. High over her they break, and round her surge and roar; and, giving place to others, moaningly depart, and dash themselves to fragments in their baffled anger: still she comes onward bravely. And though the eager multitude crowd thick and fast upon her all the night, and dawn of day discovers the untiring train yet bearing down upon the ship in an eternity of troubled water, onward she comes, with dim lights burning in her hull, and people there, asleep: as if no deadly element were peering in at every seam and chink, and no drowned seaman's grave, with but a plank to cover it, were yawning in the unfathomable depths below.

Dickens.

LOVE'S YOUNG DREAM.

OH! the days are gone when beauty bright
    My heart's chain wove ;
When my dream of life, from morn till night,
    Was love, still love !
      New hope may bloom,
      And days may come,
    Of milder, calmer beam,
But there 's nothing half so sweet in life
    As love's young dream !
Oh! there 's nothing half so sweet in life
    As love's young dream !

Though the bard to purer fame may soar,
    When wild youth 's past ;
Though he win the wise, who frown'd before,
    To smile at last ;
      He 'll never meet
      A joy so sweet
    In all his noon of fame
As when first he sung to woman's ear
    His soul-felt flame,
And at every close she blush'd to hear
    The one loved name !

Oh! that hallow'd form is ne'er forgot,
    Which first love traced ;
Still it lingering haunts the greenest spot
    On memory's waste !
      'Twas odour fled
      As soon as shed ;
    'Twas morning's wingèd dream ;
'Twas a light that ne'er can shine again
    On life's dull stream !
Oh! 'twas a light that ne'er can shine again
    On life's dull stream !

Moore.

K

APOPHTHEGMS AND APHORISMS.

OF Law there can be no less acknowledged than that her seat is the bosom of God; her voice the harmony of the world: all things in heaven and earth do her homage; the very least as feeling her care, and the greatest as not exempted from her power: both angels and men, and creatures of what condition soever, though each in different sort and manner, yet all with uniform consent, admiring her as the mother of peace and joy.   *Hooker.*

Be merry, but with modesty; be sober, but not sullen: be valiant, but not venturous: let your clothes be comely, but not costly: your diet wholesome, but not excessive: mistrust no man without cause, neither be thou credulous without proof. Serve God, fear God, love God, and God will so bless you as either your heart can wish or your friends desire.   *Lyly.*

Books, such as are worthy the name of books, ought to have no patrons but truth and sense.   *Bacon.*

For a man to write well, there are required three necessaries,—to read the best authors, observe the best speakers, and much exercise of his own style.   *Jonson.*

A good memory is the best monument. Others are subject to casualty or time; and we know that the Pyramids themselves, doting with age, have forgotten the names of their founders.   *Fuller.*

Envy is that dark shadow ever waiting upon a shining merit. *Fuller.*

Poverty wants some, Luxury many, Avarice all things.   *Cowley.*

The liberty of a people consists in being governed by laws which they have made themselves; the liberty of a private man in being master of his own time and actions, as far as may consist with the laws of God and of his country.   *Cowley.*

Aversion from proof is not wise. It is a mark of a little mind. A great man can afford to lose; a little insignificant fellow is afraid of being snuffed out.   *Cecil.*

If you choose to represent the various parts in life by holes upon a table, of different shapes—some circular, some triangular, some square, some oblong—and the persons acting these parts by bits of wood of similar shapes, we shall generally find that the triangular person has got into the square hole, the oblong into the triangular, and a square person has squeezed himself into a round hole. *Sydney Smith.*

To be wise too late, is the exactest definition of a fool. *Young.*

She—the Roman Catholic Church—may still exist in undiminished vigour, when some traveller from New Zealand, in the midst of a vast solitude, takes his stand on a broken arch of London Bridge to sketch the ruins of St Paul's. *Macaulay.*

The ceremonial of the world is not without its use : it may indeed take from warmth of friendship, but it covers the coldness of indifference.
Mackenzie.

He that begins without reason, hath reason enough to leave off, by perceiving he had no reason to begin. *Taylor.*

To be humble to superiors is duty; to equals is courtesy ; to inferiors is nobleness; and to all is safety : it being a virtue, that, for all her lowliness, commandeth the souls it stoops to.

Difficulties spur us whenever they do not check us. *Reade.*

The stage is a supplement to the pulpit, where virtue, according to Plato's sublime idea, moves our love and affection when made visible to the eye. *Disraeli.*

Where preferment goes more by favour than by merit, the rejected have more honour than the elected. *Fuller.*

The bread of life is love ; the salt of life is work ; the sweetness of life, poesy ; the water of life, faith. *Jameson.*

Plain truths lose much of their weight when they are rarefied into subtilties ; and their strength is impaired when they are spun into too fine a thread. *Stillingfleet.*

When religion is made a science, there is nothing more intricate ; when it is made a duty, nothing more easy. *Wilson.*

THE ANTIQUARY AT MARKET.

THE Antiquary led the way to the sands. Upon the links or downs
close to them, were seen four or five huts inhabited by fishers, whose
boats, drawn high upon the beach, left the odoriferous vapours of pitch
melting under a burning sun, to contend with those of the offals of fish
and other nuisances, usually collected round Scottish cottages. Undis-

turbed by these complicated steams of abomination, a middle-aged woman, with a face which had defied a thousand storms, sat mending a net at the door of one of the cottages. A handkerchief close bound about her head, and a coat which had formerly been that of a man, gave her a masculine air, which was increased by her strength, uncommon stature, and harsh voice. "What are ye for the day, your honour?" she said, or rather screamed, to Oldbuck; "caller haddocks and whitings—a bannock-fluke and a cock-paddle."

" How much for the bannock-fluke and cock-paddle?" demanded the Antiquary.

" Four white shillings and saxpence," answered the Naiad.

" Four devils and six of their imps!" retorted the Antiquary: " do ye think I am mad, Maggie!"

"And div ye think," rejoined the virago, setting her arms a-kimbo, " that my man and my sons are to gae to the sea in weather like yestreen and the day—sic a sea as it's yet outby—and get naething for their fish, and be misca'd into the bargain, Monkbarns? It's no fish ye 're buying —it's men's lives."

" Well, Maggie, I'll bid you fair—I'll bid you a shilling for the fluke and the cock-paddle, or sixpence separately—and if all your fish are as well paid, I think your man, as you call him, and your sons, will make a good voyage."

" Deil gin their boat were knocket against the Bell-rock rather! it wad be better, and the bonnier voyage o' the twa. A shilling for thae twa bonny fish! Od, that's ane indeed!"

" Well, well, you old beldame, carry your fish up to Monkbarns, and see what my sister will give you for them."

" Na, na, Monkbarns, deil a fit—I'll rather deal wi' yoursell; for, though you 're near enough, yet Miss Grizel has an unco close grip—I'll gie ye them (in a softened tone) for three-and-saxpence."

" Eighteen-pence, or nothing!"

" Eighteen-pence!!!" (in a loud tone of astonishment, which declined into a sort of rueful whine, when the dealer turned as if to walk away)— " Ye'll no be for the fish then?"—(then louder, as she saw him moving off)—" I'll gie them—and—and—and a half-a-dozen o' partans to make the sauce, for three shillings and a dram."

"Half-a-crown then, Maggie, and a dram."

"Aweel, your honour maun hae't your ain gate, nae doubt; but a dram's worth siller now—the distilleries is no working."

"And I hope they'll never work again in my time," said Oldbuck.

"Ay, ay—it's easy for your honour, and the like o' you gentle-folks, to say sae, that hae stouth and routh, and fire and fending, and meat and claith, and sit dry and canny by the fireside—but an ye wanted fire, and meat, and dry claise, and were deeing o' cauld, and had a sair heart, whilk is warst ava', wi' just tippence in your pouch, wadna ye be glad to buy a dram wi't, to be eilding and claise, and a supper and heart's ease into the bargain, till the morn's morning?"

"It's even too true an apology, Maggie. Is your goodman off to sea this morning, after his exertions last night?"

"In troth he is, Monkbarns; he was awa this morning by four o'clock, when the sea was working like barm wi' yestreen's wind, and our bit coble dancing in't like a cork.'

"Well, he's an industrious fellow. Carry the fish up to Monkbarns."

"That I will—or I'll send little Jenny, she'll rin faster; but I'll ca' on Miss Grizzy for the dram mysell, and say ye sent me."

A nondescript animal, which might have passed for a mermaid, as it was paddling in a pool among the rocks, was summoned ashore by the shrill screams of its dam; and having been made decent, as her mother called it, which was performed by adding a short red cloak to a petticoat, which was at first her sole covering, and which reached scantily below her knee, the child was dismissed with the fish in a basket, and a request on the part of Monkbarns, that they might be prepared for dinner. "It would have been long," said Oldbuck, with much self-complacency, "ere my woman-kind could have made such a reasonable bargain with that old skinflint, though they sometimes wrangle with her for an hour together under my study window, like three sea-gulls screaming and spluttering in a gale of wind."   *   *Scott.*

THE ACADEMY AT LEGADO.

IN the school of political projectors I was but ill entertained; the professors appearing, in my judgment, wholly out of their senses, which is a scene that never fails to make me melancholy. These unhappy people were proposing schemes for persuading monarchs to choose favourites upon the score of their wisdom, capacity, and virtue; of teaching ministers to consult the public good; of rewarding merit, great abilities, and eminent services; of instructing princes to know their true interest, by placing it on the same foundation with that of their people; of choosing for employments persons qualified to exercise them; with many other wild, impossible chimeras, that never entered before into the heart of man to conceive; and confirmed in me the old observation, "That there is nothing so extravagant and irrational, which some philosophers have not maintained for truth."

I heard a very warm debate between two professors about the most commodious and effectual ways and means of raising money without grieving the subject. The first affirmed, "The justest method would be to lay a certain tax upon vices and folly; and the sum fixed upon every man to be rated, after the fairest manner, by a jury of his neighbours." The second was of opinion directly contrary: "To tax those qualities of body and mind for which men chiefly value themselves; the rate to be more or less according to the degrees of excelling, the decision whereof should be left entirely to their own breast." The highest tax was upon men who are the greatest favourites of the other sex. Wit, valour, and politeness, were likewise proposed to be largely taxed, and collected in the same manner, by every person's giving his own word for the quantum of what he possessed. But as to honour, justice, wisdom, and learning, they should not be taxed at all, because they are qualifications of so singular a kind, that no man will either allow them in his neighbour, or value them in himself.

The women were proposed to be taxed according to their beauty and skill in dressing, wherein they had the same privilege with the men, to be determined by their own judgment. But constancy, good sense, and good nature, were not rated, because they would not bear the charge of collecting.　　　　　　　　　　　　　　　　　　　　　　　　　*Swift.*

SEVEN AGES OF MAN.

    ALL the world's a stage,
And all the men and women merely players:
They have their exits and their entrances ;
And one man in his time plays many parts,
His acts being seven ages. At first the infant,
Mewling and puking in the nurse's arms:
And then the whining schoolboy, with his satchel
And shining morning face, creeping like snail
Unwillingly to school : and then the lover,
Sighing like furnace, with a woful ballad
Made to his mistress' eyebrow : then a soldier,
Full of strange oaths, and bearded like the pard,
Jealous in honour, sudden and quick in quarrel,
Seeking the bubble reputation
Even in the cannon's mouth : and then the justice,
In fair round belly with good capon lined,
With eyes severe, and beard of formal cut,
Full of wise saws and modern instances,
And so he plays his part. The sixth age shifts
Into the lean and slipper'd pantaloon,
With spectacles on nose, and pouch on side ;
His youthful hose, well saved, a world too wide
For his shrunk shanks ; and his big manly voice,
Turning again toward childish treble, pipes
And whistles in his sound. Last scene of all,
That ends this strange eventful history,
Is second childishness, and mere oblivion,—
Sans teeth, sans eyes, sans taste, sans everything.

                       Shakespeare.

ANGER.

1. ANGER is a professed enemy to counsel; it is a direct storm, in which no man can be heard to speak or call from without: for if you counsel gently, you are despised: if you urge it and be vehement, you provoke it more. 2. Of all passions it endeavours most to make reason useless. 3. That it is a universal passion, of an infinite object: for no man was ever so amorous as to love a toad; none so envious, as to repine at the condition of the miserable; no man so timorous as to fear a dead bee; but anger is troubled at every thing, and every man, and every accident: and therefore, unless it be suppressed, it will make a man's condition restless. 4. If it proceeds from a great cause, it turns to fury; if from a small cause, it is peevishness: and so is always either terrible or ridiculous. 5. It is neither manly nor ingenuous. 6. It proceeds from softness of spirit and pusillanimity; which makes, that women are more angry than men, sick persons more than the healthful, old men more than young unprosperous and calamitous people than the blessed and fortunate. 7. It is troublesome, not only to those that suffer it, but to them that behold it; there being no greater incivility of entertainment, than, for the cook's fault or the negligence of the servants, to be cruel or outrageous, or unpleasant in the presence of guests. 8. It makes marriage to be a necessary and unavoidable trouble; friendships, and societies, and familiarities to be intolerable. 9. It multiplies the evils of drunkenness, and makes the levities of wine to run into madness. 10. It makes innocent jesting to be the beginning of tragedies. 11. It turns friendship into hatred; it makes a man lose himself, and his reason, and his argument in disputations. It changes discipline into tediousness and hatred of liberal institutions. It makes a prosperous man to be envied, and the unfortunate to be unpitied. It is a confluence of all the irregular passions: there is in it envy and sorrow, fear and scorn, pride and prejudice, rashness and inconsideration, rejoicing in evil and a desire to inflict it, self-love, impatience, and curiosity. And, lastly, though it be very troublesome to others, yet it is most troublesome to him that hath it.

Jeremy Taylor.

THE HOLLY TREE.

O READER! hast thou ever stood to see
       The Holly Tree?
The eye that contemplates it well perceives
       Its glossy leaves,
Ordered by an Intelligence so wise,
As might confound the Atheist's sophistries.

Below, a circling fence, its leaves are seen
       Wrinkled and keen:
No grazing cattle through their prickly round
       Can reach to wound;
But, as they grow where nothing is to fear,
Smooth and unarmed the pointless leaves appear.

I love to view these things with curious eyes,
       And moralise;
And in this wisdom of the Holly Tree
       Can emblems see,
Wherewith perchance to make a pleasant rhyme,
One which may profit in the after-time.

Thus, though abroad perchance I might appear
       Harsh and austere;
To those, who on my leisure would intrude,
       Reserved and rude;—
Gentle at home amid my friends I'd be,
Like the high leaves upon the Holly Tree.

And should my youth, as youth is apt I know,
       Some harshness show,
All vain asperities I day by day
       Would wear away,
Till the smooth temper of my age should be
Like the high leaves upon the Holly Tree.

And as when all the summer trees are seen
    So bright and green,
The Holly leaves a sober hue display
    Less bright than they ;
But, when the bare and wintry woods we see,
What then so cheerful as the Holly Tree ?

So serious should my youth appear among
    The thoughtless throng ;
So would I seem amid the young and gay
    More grave than they ;
That in my age as cheerful I might be
As the green winter of the Holly Tree.

                                        Southey.

─ ·ᘜᘉᘕᘧᘍ· ─

JEHOVAH THE PROVIDER.

AUTHOR of being ! life-sustaining King !
    Lo ! Want's dependent eye from Thee implores
The seasons, which provide nutritious stores ;
Give to her prayers the renovating spring,
And summer-heats all perfecting that bring
    The fruits which autumn from a thousand stores
    Selecteth provident ! when Earth adores
Her God, and all her vales exulting sing.
Without Thy blessing, the submissive steer
    Bends to the ploughman's galling yoke in vain ;
Without Thy blessing on the varied year,
    Can the swarth reaper grasp the golden grain ?
Without Thy blessing, all is black and drear ;
    With it, the joys of Eden bloom again.

                                        Wordsworth.

WAITING FOR THE FOE.

A T dusky eve, the rockbound headland swarms
   With crowds of eager watchers.   Anxiously,

And with bated breath, they scan the sea-board
For the expected foe. The round red sun
Has sunk into the west : the light of day
Is shrouded in the deep gray shadows of
Approaching night ; and, with glare of torchlight,
And vivid flame of startling beacon fire,
The hardy Britons cleave the murky air,
And cast their glances o'er the wat'ry course.
Each warrior bold, 'mid mingled hope and fear,
Strains eyes and ears in eagerness to gain
First tidings of the invading galleys
Of the Norsemen.
    With hand upraised, the chief
Peers out into the blackness, and beholds
In fancy what his heart doth prompt. Banners
Of the foe! The Raven black of Norway,
With wings outspread, as if on carnage bent,
And the warlike hosts of Haco and the
Norsemen of the Isles.

.   .   .   .   .   .

Or ere the space of many days had passed—
Th' October moon its advent scarce had made-
When Haco's hosts bore down upon the coast.
His warriors grim, in numbers far outshone
The hardy Scots who clustered on the shore,
And vict'ry seemed within his easy grasp.
But ere that consummation could be gained,
There came a power, which quickly changed the scene :
The God of Battles loosed His thunderbolts—
The lightnings flashed, and heaven's artill'ry,
With storm tempestuous and raging winds
Spread ravage dire throughout the Norseman's fleet :
And in a few brief hours were wrecked
The Hundred Ships that late were Norway's pride !

—A Fragment suggested by the Battle of Largs, 1263.

TO A MOUSE,

ON TURNING UP HER NEST WITH THE PLOUGH, NOVEMBER 1785.

WEE, sleekit, cowrin', tim'rous beastie,
    Oh, what a panic's in thy breastie !
Thou needna start awa' sae hasty,
        Wi' bickering brattle !
I wad be laith to rin and chase thee,
        Wi' murd'ring pattle !

I 'm truly sorry man's dominion
Has broken nature's social union,
And justifies that ill opinion
        Which maks thee startle
At me, thy poor earth-born companion,
        And fellow-mortal !

I doubt na, whyles, but thou may thieve ;
What then ? poor beastie, thou maun live !
A daimen icker in a thrave
        'S a sma' request :
I 'll get a blessin' wi' the lave,
        And never miss 't !

Thy wee bit housie, too, in ruin !
Its silly wa's the win's are strewin' !
And naething now to big a new ane
        O' foggage green !
And bleak December's winds ensuin',
        Baith snell and keen !

Thou saw the fields laid bare and waste,
And weary winter comin' fast

And cozie here, beneath the blast,
      Thou thought to dwell,
Till, crash! the cruel coulter past
      Out through thy cell.

That wee bit heap o' leaves and stibble
Has cost thee mony a weary nibble!
Now thou's turn'd out for a' thy trouble,
      But house or hauld,
To thole the winter's sleety dribble,
      And cranreuch cauld!

But, Mousie, thou art no thy lane,
In proving foresight may be vain:
The best laid schemes o' mice and men
      Gang aft a-gley,
And lea'e us nought but grief and pain
      For promised joy.

Still thou art blest, compared wi' me!
The present only toucheth thee:
But, oh! I backward cast my ee
      On prospects drear!
And forward, though I canna see,
      I guess and fear.   *Burns.*

LIFE.

LIFE! what is life? A shadow!
    Its date is but the immediate breath we draw;
Nor have we surety for a second gale:
Ten thousand accidents in ambush lie,
A frail and fickle tenement it is,
Which, like the brittle glass that measures time,
Is often broke, ere half it sands are run.   *Jones.*

M

THE BRAHMIN AND THE KNAVES.

AN EASTERN APOLOGUE.

A PIOUS Brahmin made a vow that on a certain day he would sacrifice a sheep, and on the appointed morning he went forth to buy one. There lived in his neighbourhood three rogues who knew of his vow, and laid a scheme for profiting by it. The first met him and said, "O Brahmin, wilt thou buy a sheep? I have one fit for sacrifice." "It is for that very purpose," said the holy man, "that I came forth this day." Then the impostor opened a bag, and brought out of it an unclean beast, an ugly dog, lame and blind. Thereon the Brahmin cried out, "Wretch, who touchest things impure, and utterest things untrue, callest thou that cur a sheep?" "Truly," answered the other, "it is a sheep of the finest fleece, and of the sweetest flesh. O Brahmin, it will be an offering most acceptable to the gods." "Friend," said the Brahmin, "either thou or I must be blind."

Just then one of the accomplices came up. " Praised be the gods," said this second rogue, " that I have been saved the trouble of going to the market for a sheep! This is such a sheep as I wanted. For how much wilt thou sell it?" When the Brahmin heard this, his mind waved to and fro, like one swinging in the air at a holy festival. " Sir," said he to the new-comer, " take heed what thou doest; this is no sheep, but an unclean cur." " O Brahmin," said the new-comer, " thou art drunk or mad!"

At this time the third confederate drew near. " Let us ask this man," said the Brahmin, "what the creature is, and I will stand by what he shall say." To this the others agreed; and the Brahmin called out, " O stranger, what dost thou call this beast?" " Surely, O Brahmin," said the knave, " it is a fine sheep." Then the Brahmin said, " Surely the gods have taken away my senses;" and he asked pardon of him who carried the dog, and bought it for a measure of rice and a pot of ghee, and offered it up to the gods, who, being wroth at this unclean sacrifice, smote him with a sore disease in all his joints.

Macaulay.

A CLUSTER OF SCOTTISH PROVERBS.

EVERY man bows to the bush he gets bield frae.
　　Keep out o' his company that cracks o' his cheatery.
Cripples are aye great doers—break your leg and try.
Mony ane speaks o' Robin Hood that ne'er shot wi' his bow.
A wise man carries his cloak in fair weather, and a fool wants his in rain.
He that doesna mind corn pickles never comes to forpits.
A crooked stick will throw a crooked shadow.
A man's weal or wae as he thinks himsel sae.
Do weel, and doubt nae man ; do ill, and doubt a' men.
A dreigh drink is better than a dry sermon.
Better be the head o' the commons than the tail o' the gentry.
" Sail," quo' the king ; " Haud," quo' the wind.
Ilka blade o' grass keps its ain drap o' dew.
" I winna mak a toil o' a pleasure," quo' the man when he buried his wife.

EPIGRAMS.

A CHANCERY SUIT.

MR LEACH made a speech, angry, neat, but wrong :
  Mr Hart, on the other part, was prosy, dull, and long.

Mr Bell spoke very well, though nobody knew about what ;
Mr Trower talked for an hour, sat down, fatigued, and hot.

Mr Parker made the case darker, which was dark enough without ;
Mr Cooke quoted his book, and the Chancellor said, " I doubt."

THE THEORY OF PECULATION.

A LITTLE stealing is a dangerous part,
  But stealing largely is a noble art ;
'Tis mean to rob a henroost, or a hen,
But stealing thousands makes us gentlemen.

ON A MAN NAMED NOTT.

THERE was a man who was Nott born,
  His father was Nott before him,
He did Nott live, he did Nott die,
And his epitaph was Nott o'er him.

A GOOSE'S REASON.

A GOOSE, my grandam one day said,
  Entering a barn, pops down its head :
I begg'd her then the cause to show ;
She told me she must wave the task,
For nothing but a goose would ask,
What nothing but a goose could know.

MARRIAGE IN HEAVEN.

SAID Celia to a reverend Dean,
  " What reason can be given,
Since marriage is a holy thing,
  That they have none in heaven ? "

" They have," says he, " no women there."
  She quick returns the jest :
" Women there are, but I'm afraid
  They cannot find a priest."

THE FORTUNATE DEFECT.

HOW like is this picture, you'd think that it breathes !
  What life ! what expression ! what spirit !
It wants but a tongue. " Alas ! " said the spouse,
  " That want is its principal merit."

THE RULE OF THE ROAD.

THE rule of the road is a paradox quite
  Both in riding and driving along ;
If you go the left you are sure to go right,
  If you go to the right you go wrong :
But in walking the streets, 'tis a different case,
  To the right it is right you should bear,
To the left should be left quite enough of free space
  For the persons you chance to meet there.

LADIES' MEN.

WHETHER tall men, or short men, are best,
  Or bold men, or modest or shy men,
I can't say ; but I this can protest,
  All the fair are in favour of *hy-men*.

AUTUMN.

SOON as the morning trembles o'er the sky,
   And unperceived, unfolds the spreading day;
Before the ripen'd field the reapers stand,
In fair array. . . . . . .
At once they stoop and swell the lusty sheaves;
While through their cheerful band the rural talk,
The rural scandal, and the rural jest,
Fly harmless, to deceive the tedious time,
And steal unfelt the sultry hours away.
Behind, the master walks, builds up the shocks :
And, conscious, glancing oft on every side
His sated eye, feels his heart heave with joy.
The gleaners spread around, and here and there,
Spike after spike, their scanty harvest pick.
Be not too narrow, husbandman! but fling
From the full sheaf, with charitable stealth,
The liberal handful.   Think, oh, think!
How good the God of harvest is to you,
Who pours abundance o'er your flowing fields;
While these unhappy partners of your kind
Wide hover round you, like the fowls of heaven,
And ask their humble dole.   The various turns
Of fortune ponder; that your sons may want
What now, with hard reluctance, faint, ye give.

Thomson.

TO-MORROW.

IN the downhill of life, when I find I'm declining,
    May my lot no less fortunate be
Than a snug elbow-chair can afford for reclining,
    And a cot that o'erlooks the white sea ;
With an ambling pad-pony to pace o'er the lawn,
    While I carol away idle sorrow,
And blithe as the lark that each day hails the dawn
    Look forward with hope for to-morrow.

With a porch at my door, both for shelter and shade too,
    As the sunshine or rain may prevail ;
And a small spot of ground for the use of the spade too,
    With a barn for the use of the flail :
A cow for my dairy, a dog for my game,
    And a purse when a friend wants to borrow ;
I'll envy no nabob his riches or fame,
    Nor what honours await him to morrow.

From the bleak northern blast may my cot be completely
    Secured by a neighbouring hill ;
And at night may repose steal upon me more sweetly
    By the sound of a murmuring rill.
And while peace and plenty I find at my board,
    With a heart free from sickness and sorrow,
With my friends may I share what to-day may afford,
    And let them spread the table to-morrow.

And when I at last must throw off this frail covering
    Which I've worn for threescore years and ten,
On the brink of the grave I'll not seek to keep hovering,
    Nor my thread wish to spin o'er again :
But my face in the glass I'll serenely survey,
    And with smiles count each wrinkle and furrow ;
As this old worn out stuff, which is thread bare to day,
    May become everlasting to morrow.   *Collins.*

N

SHAKESPEARE AND HIS WRITINGS.

SHAKESPEARE may now begin to assume the dignity of an ancient,
and claim the privilege of established fame and prescriptive venera-
tion. He has long outlived his century, the term commonly fixed as the
test of literary merit. Whatever advantages he might once derive from
personal allusions, local customs, or temporary opinions, have for many
years been lost; and every topic of merriment or motive of sorrow which
the motives of artificial life afforded him, now only obscure the scenes
which they once illuminated. The effects of favour and competition are
at an end; the tradition of his friendships and his enmities has perished;
his works support no opinion with arguments, nor supply any faction with
invectives; they can neither indulge vanity nor gratify malignity, but are
read without any other reason than the desire of pleasure, and are therefore praised only as pleasure is obtained; yet, thus unassisted by interest
or passion, they have passed through variations of taste and changes of
manners, and, as they devolved from one generation to another, have
received new honours at every transmission.

Shakespeare is, above all writers, at least above all modern writers, the
poet of nature—the poet that holds up to his readers a faithful mirror of
manners and of life. His characters are not modified by the customs of
particular places, unpractised by the rest of the world; by the peculiarities
of studies or professions, which can operate but upon small numbers; or
by the accidents of transient fashions or temporary opinions: they are
the genuine progeny of common humanity, such as the world will always
supply and observation will always find. His persons act and speak by
the influence of those general passions and principles by which all minds
are agitated, and the whole system of life is continued in motion. In the
writings of other poets, a character is too often an individual; in those of
Shakespeare it is commonly a species.

It is from this wide extension of design that so much instruction is
derived. It is this which fills the plays of Shakespeare with practical
axioms and domestic wisdom. It was said of Euripides that every verse
was a precept; and it may be said of Shakespeare that from his works may
be collected a system of civil and economical prudence; yet his real power

is not shown in the splendour of particular passages, but by the progress of his fable and the tenor of his dialogue; and he that tries to recommend him by select quotations, will succeed like the pedant in Hierocles, who, when he offered his house to sale, carried a brick in his pocket as a specimen.

It will not easily be imagined how much Shakespeare excels in accommodating his sentiments to real life, but by comparing him with other authors. It was observed of the ancient schools of declamation, that the more diligently they were frequented, the more was the student disqualified for the world, because he found nothing there which he should ever meet in any other place. The same remark may be applied to every stage but that of Shakespeare. The theatre, when it is under any other direction, is peopled by such characters as were never seen, conversing in a language which was never heard, upon topics which will never arise in the commerce of mankind. But the dialogue of this author is often so evidently determined by the incident which produces it, and is pursued with so much ease and simplicity, that it seems scarcely to claim the merit of fiction, but to have been gleaned by diligent selection out of common conversation and common occurrences.

This, therefore, is the praise of Shakespeare, that his drama is the mirror of life; that he who has mazed his imagination in following the phantoms which other writers raise up before him, may here be cured of his delirious ecstacies by reading human sentiments in human language; by scenes by which a hermit may estimate the transactions of the world, and a confessor predict the progress of the passions. *Johnson.*

CONTENTMENT.

I KNEW a man that had health and riches, and several houses, all beautiful and ready furnished, and would often trouble himself and family to be removing from one house to another; and being asked by a friend why he removed so often from one house to another, replied, " It was to find content in some of them." But his friend, knowing his temper, told him, " If he would find content in any of his houses, he must leave himself behind him; for content will never dwell but in a meek and quiet soul." And this may appear, if we read and consider what our Saviour says in St Matthew's Gospel, for He there says, " Blessed be the merciful, for they shall obtain mercy. Blessed be the pure in heart, for they shall see God. Blessed be the poor in spirit, for theirs is the kingdom of heaven. And blessed be the meek, for they shall possess the earth." Not that the meek shall not also obtain mercy, and see God, and be comforted, and at last come to the kingdom of heaven; but, in the meantime, he, and he only, possesses the earth, as he goes toward that kingdom of kingdoms, by being humble and cheerful, and content with what his good God has allotted him. He has no turbulent, repining, vexatious thoughts that he deserves better; nor is vexed when he sees others possessed of more honour or more riches than his wise God has allotted for his share; but he possesses what he has with a meek and contented quietness, such a quietness as makes his very dreams pleasing, both to God and himself.

Walton.

THE BIBLE.

WITHIN this awful volume lies
　　The mystery of mysteries :
Happiest they of human race
To whom their God has given grace
To read, to fear, to hope, to pray,
To lift the latch—to force the way ;
But better had they ne'er been born
Who read to doubt, or read to scorn. 　　*Scott.*

THE TWA SISTERS.

THERE were twa sisters lived in a bouir;
Binnorie, O Binnorie;
The youngest o' them, oh, she was a flouir!
By the bonnie mill-dams o' Binnorie.

There came a squire frae the west;
Binnorie, O Binnorie;
He lo'ed them baith, but the youngest best.
By the bonnie mill dams o' Binnorie.

He gied the eldest a gay gold ring;
But he lo'ed the youngest abune a' thing.

He courted the eldest wi' broach and knife ;
But he lo'ed the youngest as his life.

The eldest she was vexèd sair,
And sore envied her sister fair.

And it fell ance upon a day,
The eldest to the youngest did say :

" Oh, sister, come to the sea strand,
And see our father's ships come to land."

She's taen her by the milk-white hand,
And led her doun to the sea strand.

The youngest sat upon a stane ;
The eldest cam' and threw her in.

" Oh, sister, sister, lend me your hand,
And you shall be heir of half my land."

" Oh, sister, I'll not reach my hand,
And I'll be heir of your land.

Shame fa' the hand that I should take !
It twined me and my world's maik.

Your cherry cheeks and yellow hair
Had gar'd me gang maiden evermair."

" Oh, sister, reach me but your glove,
And you shall be sweet William's love.

" Sink on, nor hope for hand or glove ;
And sweet William shall better be my love."

First she sank, and syne she swam,
Until she cam to Tweed mill-dam.

The miller's daughter was baking breid,
And gaed for water as she had need.

" Oh, father, father, in our mill-dam,
There 's either a ladye or a milk-white swan."

The miller quickly drew his dam,
And there he fand a drown'd woman.

You couldna see her yellow hair,
For gowd and pearls that were sae rare.

You couldna see her middle sma',
Her gowden girdle was sae braw.

You couldna see her lilie feet,
Her gowden fringes were sae deep.

You couldna see her fingers sma' ;
Wi' diamond rings they were cover'd a'.

" Sair will they be, whae'er they be,
The hearts that live to weep for thee !"

Then by there cam' a harper fine,
That harpèd to the king at dine.

And when he look'd that lady on,
He sigh'd and made a heavy moan.

He has ta'en three locks o' her yellow hair,
And wi' them strung his harp sae fair.

And he brought the harp to her father's hall,
And there the court was assembled all.

He laid this harp upon a stone,
And straight it began to play alone.

" Oh yonder sits my father, the king !
And yonder sits my mother, the queen !

" And yonder stands my brother Hugh,
And by him my William sweet and true : "

But the last tune that the harp play'd then,
     Binnorie, O Binnorie,
Was, " Woe to my sister, false Helen ! "
     By the bonnie mill-dams o' Binnorie.

MR PEPYS QUARRELS WITH HIS WIFE.

MAY 11, 1667.—My wife being dressed this day in fair hair, did make me so mad, that I spoke not one word to her, though I was ready to burst with anger. After that, Creed and I into the Park, and walked, a most pleasant evening, and so took coach, and took up my wife, and in my way home discovered my trouble to my wife for her white locks, swearing several times, which I pray God forgive me for, and bending my fist, that I would not endure it. She, poor wretch, was surprised with it, and made me no answer all the way home; but there we parted. and I to the office late, and then home, and without supper to bed. vexed.

12. (Lord's Day.)—Up and to my chamber, to settle some accounts there, and by and by down comes my wife to me in her night gown, and we began calmly, that, upon having money to lace her gown for second mourning, she would promise to wear white locks no more in my sight, which I, like a severe fool, thinking not enough, began to except against, and made her fly out to very high terms and cry, and in her heat, told me of keeping company with Mrs Knipp, saying, that if I would promise never to see her more—of whom she had more reason to suspect than I had heretofore of Pembleton—she would never wear white locks more. This vexed me, but I restrained myself from saying anything, but do think never to see this woman—at least, to have here more; and so all very good friends as ever. My wife and I bethought ourselves to go to a French house to dinner, and so inquired out Monsieur Robins, my periwig-maker, who keeps an ordinary, and in an ugly street in Covent Garden did find him at the door, and so we in; and in a moment almost had the table covered, and clean glasses, and all in the French manner, and a mess of potage first, and then a piece of bœuf-à-la-mode, all exceeding well-seasoned, and to our great liking; at least it would have been anywhere else but in this bad street, and in a periwig-maker's house; but to see the pleasant and ready attendance that we had, and all things so desirous to please, and ingenious in the people, did take me mightily. Our dinner cost us 6s. *Pepys.*

MORNING.

LOOK where the Morn, in russet mantle clad,
  Walks o'er the dew of yon high eastern hill.

            Look what streaks
Do lace the severing clouds in yonder east.
Night's tapers are burnt out, and jocund Day
Stands tiptoe on the misty mountain tops.

The glowworm shows the matin to be near,
And 'gins to pale his ineffectual fire.

The wolves have prey'd; and, look, the gentle Day,
Before the wheels of Phœbus, round about,
Dapples the drowsy east with spots of gray.

Shakespeare.

NIGHT.

O MAJESTIC Night!
 Nature's great ancestor! Day's elder born!
And fated to survive the transient sun!
By mortals and immortals seen with awe.
A starry crown thy raven brow adorns;
An azure zone thy waist: clouds, in heaven's loom
Wrought through varieties of shape and shade,
In ample folds of drapery divine,
Thy flowing mantle form, and, heaven throughout,
Voluminously pour thy pompous train:
Thy gloomy grandeurs—Nature's most august,
Inspiring aspect!—claim a grateful verse,
And, like a sable curtain starr'd with gold,
Drawn o'er my labours past, shall clothe the scene.

Young.

PARTIAL JUSTICE.

THERE is a village (no matter where) in which the inhabitants, on
one day in the year, sit down to a dinner prepared at the common
expense : by an extraordinary piece of tyranny, (which Lord Hawkesbury
would call the wisdom of the village ancestors,) the inhabitants of three
of the streets, about a hundred years ago, seized upon the inhabitants of
the fourth street, bound them hand and foot, laid them upon their backs,
and compelled them to look on while the rest were stuffing themselves
with beef and beer : the next year, the inhabitants of the persecuted street
(though they contributed an equal quota of the expense) were treated
precisely in the same manner. The tyranny grew into a custom; and (as
the manner of our nature is) it was considered as the most sacred of all
duties to keep these poor fellows without their annual dinner : the village
was so tenacious of this practice, that nothing could induce them to resign
it : every enemy to it was looked upon as a disbeliever in Divine Provi-
dence, and any nefarious churchwarden who wished to succeed in his
election, had nothing to do but to represent his antagonist as an aboli-
tionist, in order to frustrate his ambition, endanger his life, and throw the
village into a state of the most dreadful commotion. By degrees, however, the obnoxious street grew to be so well peopled, and its inhabitants
so firmly united, that their oppressors, more afraid of injustice, were more
disposed to be just. At the next dinner they are unbound, the year after
allowed to sit upright, then a bit of bread and a glass of water; till at last,
after a long series of concessions, they are emboldened to ask, in pretty
plain terms, that they may be allowed to sit down at the bottom of the
table, and to fill their bellies as well as the rest. Forthwith a general cry
of shame and scandal. " Ten years ago, were you not laid upon your
backs? Don't you remember what a great thing you thought it to get a
piece of bread? How thankful you were for cheese-parings? Have you
forgotten that memorable era, when the lord of the manor interfered to
obtain for you a slice of the public pudding? And now, with an audacity
only equalled by your ingratitude, you have the impudence to ask for
knives and forks, and to request, in terms too plain to be mistaken, that
you may sit down to table with the rest, and be indulged even with beef

and beer: there are not more than half-a-dozen dishes which we have reserved for ourselves: the rest has been thrown open to you in the utmost profusion; you have potatoes and carrots, suet dumplings, sops in the pan, and delicious toast and water, in incredible quantities. Beef, mutton, lamb, pork, and veal are ours; and if you were not the most restless and dissatisfied of human beings, you would never think of aspiring to enjoy them."

Is not this, my dainty Abraham, the very nonsense, and the very insult which is talked to and practised upon the Catholics? You are surprised that men who have tasted of partial justice should ask for perfect justice; that he who has been robbed of coat and cloak will not be contented with the restitution of one of his garments. He would be a very lazy blockhead if he were content; and I (who, though an inhabitant of the village, have preserved, thank God, some sense of justice) most earnestly counsel these half-fed claimants to persevere in their just demands till they are admitted to a more complete share of a dinner for which they pay as much as the others; and if they see a little attenuated lawyer squabbling at the head of their opponents, let them desire him to empty his pockets, and to pull out all the pieces of duck, fowl, and pudding which he has filched from the public feast, to carry home to his wife and children.

Sydney Smith.

TASTE AND FEELING.

THE French have taste in all they do,
  Which we are quite without;
For Nature, which to them gave *goût*,
  To us gave only *gout.*

ANSWER.

Condemn not in such haste,
  To letters four appealing;
French *goût* is only *taste*,
  But English *gout* is feeling!

SONG OF SELMA.

CRATH son of Odgal repined; his brother had been slain by Armar. He came disguised like a son of the sea; fair was his skiff on the wave : white his locks of age; calm his serious brow. Fairest of women, he said, loveliest daughter of Armin ! a rock not distant in the sea bears a tree on its side; red shines the fruit afar ! There Armar waits for Daura. I come to carry his love! She went, she called on Armar. Nought answered, but the son of the rock, Armar, my love! why tormentest thou me with fear! hear, son of Arnart, hear; it is Daura, who calleth thee ! Erath the traitor fled laughing to the land. She lifted up her voice; she called for her brother and her father. Arindal! Armin! none to relieve your Daura !

Her voice came over the sea. Arindal my son descended from the hill ; rough in spoils of the chase. His arrows rattled by his side ; his bow was in his hand ; five dark-gray dogs attend his steps. He saw fierce Erath on the shore ; he seized and bound him to an oak. Thick wind the thongs of the hide around his limbs ; he loads the wind with his groans. Arindal ascends the deep in his boat, to bring Daura to land. Armar came in his wrath, and let fly the gray-feathered shaft. It sunk, it sunk in thy heart, O Arindal my son ; for Erath the traitor thou diedst. The oar is stopped at once ; he panted on the rock and expired. What is thy grief, O Daura, when round thy feet is poured thy brother's blood ! The boat is broken in twain. Armar plunges into the sea, to rescue his Daura, or die. Sudden a blast from the hill came over the waves. He sunk, and he rose no more.

Alone, on the sea-beat rock, my daughter was heard to complain. All night I heard her cries, loud was the wind, the rain beat hard on the hill. Before morning appeared, her voice was weak. It died away, like the evening breeze among the grass of the rocks. Spent with grief, she ex-pired ; and left thee, Armin, alone. Often by the setting moon I see the ghosts of my children. Half viewless they walk in mournful conference together. Will none of you speak in pity? They do not regard their father. I am sad, O Carmor, nor small is my cause of woe !

Ossian.

THE DEVIL'S WALK.

FROM his brimstone bed, at break of day,
    A-walking the Devil has gone,
To visit his snug little farm of the earth,
    And see how his stock goes on.

And over the hill, and over the dale,
    He walk'd, and over the plain;
And backwards and forwards he switch'd his long tail,
    As a gentleman switches his cane.

And pray how was the Devil drest?
    Oh! he was in his Sunday's best:
His coat was red, and his breeches were blue,
    With a hole behind, where his tail came through.

He saw a lawyer killing a viper
  On a dunghill, beside his own stable ;
And the Devil smiled, for it put him in mind
  Of Cain and his brother Abel.

An apothecary, on a white horse,
  Rode by on his avocations :
" Oh !" says the Devil, " there's my old friend
  Death in the Revelations !"

He saw a cottage, with a double coach-house,
  A cottage of gentility !
And the Devil was pleased, for his darling vice
  Is the pride that apes humility.

He stepp'd into a rich bookseller's shop ;
  Says he, " We are both of one college,
For I myself sat, like a cormorant, once,
  Hard by on the tree of knowledge."

As he pass'd through Cold-Bath-Fields, he saw
  A solitary cell :
And the Devil was charm'd, for it gave him a hint
  For improving the prisons of hell.

He saw a turnkey in a trice
  Fetter a troublesome jade !
" Ah ! nimble," quoth he, " do the fingers move
  When they're used to their trade."

He saw the same turnkey unfetter the same,
  But with little expedition ;
And the Devil thought on the long debates
  On the Slave Trade Abolition.

Down the river did glide, with wind and with tide,
 A pig, with vast celerity !
And the Devil grinn'd, for he saw all the while
How it cut its own throat, and he thought with a smile
 Of " England's commercial prosperity ! "

 He saw a certain minister
  (A minister to his mind)
 Go up into a certain house,
  With a majority behind.

 The Devil quoted Genesis,
  Like a very learned clerk,
 How " Noah, and his creeping things,
  Went up into the ark ! "

General Gascoigne's burning face
 He saw with consternation,
And back to hell his way did take ;
For the Devil thought, by a slight mistake,
 'Twas the General Conflagration !

Porson.

PRIDE OF AUTHORSHIP.

" I AM going to fly," cried the gigantic ostrich ; and the whole assembly
of birds gathered round in earnest expectation. " I am going to
fly," he cried again ; and, stretching out his immense pinions, he shot, like
a ship with outspread sails, away over the ground, without, however, rising
an inch above it. Thus it happens when a notion of being poetical takes
possession of unpoetical brains ; in the opening of their monstrous odes
they boast of their intention to soar over clouds and stars, but never-
theless remain constant to the dust. ;

Lessing.

THE CAPTIVE.

IN prison strong, to massive wall enchain'd ;
   Fetter'd in hands and feet—in heart and soul ;
The youthful captive hangs his troubled head,
   While sad reflections through his mem'ry roll.

Thoughts of home, of happiness, of friends,—
Of country loved, and freedom's voice now hush'd,
Of glorious future fondly conjured up;
But now, alas! by war's sad havoc crush'd.

Condemn'd to die! Yet not afraid of death!
Nay, proud that he is martyr to the cause
Of freedom. And in high heaven he hopes
As life's last moment near him draws.

RUSSIAN WATCHMAN'S SONG.

H EARKEN, folks, to what I'm singing—
Ten o'clock the bell is ringing:
Ten commandments were from heaven
By th' Almighty to us given.
Ill our watching would defend you,
Did not God himself befriend you;
Fount of goodness, power, and might,
Give to all a happy night!

LACONICS.

F EAR sometimes adds wings to the heels, and sometimes nails them to the ground, and fetters them from moving. *Montaigne.*

A poet hurts himself by writing prose; as a race-horse hurts his motions by condescending to draw in a team. *Shenstone.*

Those beings only are fit for solitude, who like nobody, are like nobody, and are liked by nobody. *Zimmerman.*

Satire is a sort of glass, wherein beholders generally discover everybody's face but their own,—which is the chief reason for that kind of reception it meets in the world, and that so very few are offended by it. *Swift.*

It is with wits as with razors, which are never so apt to cut those they are employed on, as when they have lost their edge. *Swift.*

THE STARTLED STAG.

THE stag at eve had drunk his fill,
   Where danced the moon on Monan's rill,
And deep his midnight lair had made
In lone Glenartney's hazel shade ;
But, when the sun his beacon red
Had kindled on Benvoirlich's head,
The deep-mouth'd bloodhound's heavy bay
Resounded up the rocky way,
And faint, from farther distance borne,
Were heard the clanging hoof and horn.

As chief who hears his warder call,
" To arms ! the foemen storm the wall,"—
The antler'd monarch of the waste
Sprung from his heathery couch in haste.
But, ere his fleet career he took,
The dew-drops from his flanks he shook ;
Like crested leader proud and high,
Toss'd his beam'd frontlet to the sky ;
A moment gazed adown the dale,
A moment snuff'd the tainted gale,
A moment listen'd to the cry,
That thicken'd as the chase drew nigh ;
Then, as the headmost foes appear'd,
With one brave bound the copse he clear'd,
And, stretching forward free and far,
Sought the wild heaths of Uam-Var.

  .   .   .   .   .

The noble stag was pausing now
Upon the mountain's southern brow
Where broad extended, far beneath,
The varied realms of fair Menteith.

With anxious eye he wander'd o'er
Mountain and meadow, moss and moor,
And ponder'd refuge from his toil,
By far Lochard or Aberfoyle.
But nearer was the copse-wood gray,
That waved and wept on Loch-Achray,
And mingled with the pine-trees blue
On the bold cliffs of Benvenue.
Fresh vigour with the hope return'd,
With flying foot the heath he spurn'd,
Held westward with unwearied race,
And left behind the panting chase.

Scott.

OMNIPRESENCE OF THE DEITY.

ALL are but parts of one stupendous whole,
Whose body nature is, and God the soul;
That, changed through all, and yet in all the same,
Great in the earth, as in th' ethereal frame,
Warms in the sun, refreshes in the breeze,
Glows in the stars, and blossoms in the trees;
Lives through all life, extends through all extent,
Spreads undivided, operates unspent;
Breathes in our soul, informs our mortal part,
As full, as perfect, in a hair as heart;
As full, as perfect, in vile man that mourns,
As the rapt seraph that adores and burns;
To Him, no high, no low, no great, no small;
He fills, He bounds, connects, and equals all.

Pope.

THE USE OF HISTORY.

TO teach and to inculcate the general principles of virtue, and the general rules of wisdom and good policy which result from such details of actions and characters, comes, for the most part, and always should come, expressly and directly into the design of those who are capable of giving such details; and, therefore, whilst they narrate as historians, they hint often as philosophers: they put into our hands, as it were, on every proper occasion, the end of a clue, that serves to remind us of searching, and to guide us in the search of that truth which the example before us either establishes or illustrates. If a writer neglects this part, we are able, however, to supply his neglect by our own attention and industry; and when he gives us a good history of Peruvians or Mexicans, of Chinese or Tartars, of Muscovites or Negroes, we may blame him, but we must blame ourselves much more, if we do not make it a good lesson of philosophy. This being the general use of history, it is not to be neglected. Every one may make it who is able to read, and to reflect on what he reads; and every one who makes it will find, in his degree, the benefit that arises from an early acquaintance contracted in this manner with mankind. We are not only passengers or sojourners in this world, but we are absolute strangers at the first steps we make in it. Our guides are often ignorant, often unfaithful. By this map of the country, which history spreads before us, we may learn, if we please, to guide ourselves. In our journey through it, we are beset on every side. We are besieged sometimes, even in our strongest holds. Terrors and temptations, conducted by the passions of other men, assault us; and our own passions, that correspond with these, betray us. History is a collection of the journals of those who have travelled through the same country, and been exposed to the same accidents; and their good and their ill success are equally instructive. In this pursuit of knowledge an immense field is opened to us: general histories, sacred and profane; the histories of particular countries, particular events, particular orders, particular men; memorials, anecdotes, travels. But we must not ramble in this field without discernment or choice, nor even with these must we ramble too long.

Bolingbroke.

MRS PARTINGTON.

I DO not mean to be disrespectful, but the attempt of the Lords to stop the progress of reform reminds me very forcibly of the great storm of Sidmouth, and of the conduct of the excellent Mrs Partington on that occasion. In the winter of 1824, there set in a great flood upon that town—the tide rose to an incredible height—the waves rushed in upon the houses, and everything was threatened with destruction! In the midst of this sublime and terrible storm, Dame Partington, who lived upon the beach, was seen at the door of her house with mop and pattens, trundling her mop, squeezing out the sea-water, and vigorously pushing away the Atlantic Ocean. The Atlantic was roused. Mrs Partington's spirit was up; but I need not tell you that the contest was unequal. The Atlantic Ocean beat Mrs Partington. She was excellent at a slop or a puddle, but she should not have meddled with a tempest. Gentlemen, be at your ease—be quiet and steady. You will beat Mrs Partington.

Sidney Smith.

LITERARY PUFFING.

MEN of letters have ceased to court individuals, and have begun to court the public. They formerly used flattery. They now use puffing. Whether the old or the new vice be the worse, whether those who formerly lavished insincere praise on others, or those who now contrive by every art of beggary and bribery to stun the public with praises of themselves, disgrace their vocation the more deeply, we shall not attempt to decide. But of this we are sure, that it is high time to make a stand against the new trickery. The puffing of books is now so shamefully and so successfully carried on, that it is the duty of all who are anxious for the purity of the national taste, or for the honour of the literary character, to join in discountenancing the practice. All the pens that ever were employed in magnifying Bish's lucky office, Romanis's fleecy hosiery, Packwood's razor strops, and Rowland's Kalydor, all the placard-bearers of Dr Eady, all the wall-chalkers of Day and Martin, seem to have taken service with the poets and novelists of this generation. Devices which in the lowest trades are considered as disreputable are adopted without scruple, and improved upon with a despicable ingenuity, by people engaged in a pursuit which never was and never will be considered as a mere trade by any man of honour and virtue. A butcher of the higher class disdains to ticket his meat. A mercer of the higher class would be ashamed to hang up papers in his window inviting the passers-by to look at the stock of a bankrupt, all of the first quality, and going for half the value. We expect some reserve, some decent pride. in our hatter and our bootmaker. But no artifice by which notoriety can be obtained is thought too abject for a man of letters.

It is amusing to think over the history of most of the publications which have had a run during the last few years. The publisher is often the publisher of some periodical work. In this periodical work the first flourish of trumpets is sounded. The peal is then echoed and re-echoed by all the other periodical works over which the publisher, or the author, or the author's coterie, may have any influence. The newspapers are for a fortnight filled with puffs of all the various kinds which Sheridan enumerated, direct, oblique, and collusive.

Macaulay.

ZARA'S EAR-RINGS.

" MY ear-rings! my ear-rings! they've dropt into the well,
    And what to say to Muça, I cannot, cannot tell."—
'Twas thus, Granada's fountain by, spoke Albuharez' daughter,—
" The well is deep, far down they lie, beneath the cold blue water—
To me did Muça give them, when he spake his sad farewell,
And what to say when he comes back, alas! I cannot tell.

" My ear-rings! my ear-rings! they were pearls in silver set,
That when my Moor was far away, I ne'er should him forget,
That I ne'er to other tongue should list, nor smile on other's tale,
But remember he my lips had kiss'd, pure as those ear-rings pale—
When he comes back and hears that I have dropp'd them in the well,
Oh, what will Muça think of me, I cannot, cannot tell.

" My ear-rings! my ear-rings! he'll say they should have been,
Not of pearl and silver, but of gold and glittering sheen,
Of jasper and of onyx, and of diamond shining clear,
Changing to the changing light, with radiance insincere—
That changeful mind unchanging gems are not befitting well—
Thus will he think,—and what to say, alas! I cannot tell.

" He'll think when I to market went, I loiter'd by the way;
He'll think a willing ear I lent to all the lads might say;
He'll think some other lover's hand among my tresses noosed,
From the ears where he had placed them, my rings of pearl unloosed;
He'll think when I was sporting so beside this marble well,
My pearls fell in,—and what to say, alas! I cannot tell.

" He'll say I am a woman, and we are all the same;
He'll say I loved when he was here to whisper of his flame—
But when he went to Tunis my virgin troth had broken,
And thought no more of Muça, and cared not for his token.
My ear-rings! my ear-rings! O luckless, luckless well!
For what to say to Muça, alas! I cannot tell.

" I 'll tell the truth to Muça, and I hope he will believe—
That I have thought of him at morning, and thought of him at eve :
That musing on my lover, when down the sun was gone,
His ear-rings in my hand I held, by the fountain all alone :
And that my mind was o'er the sea, when from my hand they fell,
And that deep his love lies in my heart, as they lie in the well."

Lockhart.

ECCENTRIC ROYAL PROMOTIONS.

MARC ANTONY gave the house of a Roman citizen to a cook who had prepared for him a good supper ! Louis XI. promoted a poor priest whom he found sleeping in the porch of a church, that the proverb might be verified, that to lucky men good fortune will come even when they are asleep. Our Henry VII. made a viceroy of Ireland, if not for the sake of, at least with a clench. When the king was told that all Ireland could not rule the Earl of Kildare, he said, Then shall this earl rule all Ireland. When Cardinal de Monte was elected pope, before he left the conclave, he bestowed a cardinal's hat upon a servant, whose chief merit consisted in the daily attentions he paid to his holiness's monkey ! George Villiers was suddenly raised from a private station, and loaded with wealth and honours by James the First, merely for his personal beauty. Almost all the favourites of James became so from their handsomeness. M. de Chamillart, Minister of France, owed his promotion merely to his being the only man who could beat Louis XIV. at billiards. The Duke of Luynes was originally a country lad, who insinuated himself into the favour of Louis XIII., then young, by making bird-traps (*pies-grièches*) to catch sparrows. It was little expected, says Voltaire, that these puerile amusements were to be terminated by a most sanguinary revolution. De Luynes, after causing his patron, the Marshal D'Ancre, to be assassinated, and the queen-mother to be imprisoned, raised himself to a title and the most tyrannical power. Sir Walter Raleigh owed his promotion to an act of gallantry to Queen Elizabeth, and Sir Christopher Hatton owed his preferment to his dancing.

Isaac Disraeli.

WINTER.

THE wintry west extends his blast,
　　And hail and rain does blaw ;
Or the stormy north sends driving forth
　　The blinding sleet and snaw :
While, tumbling brown, the burn comes down,
　　And roars frae bank to brae ;
And bird and beast in covert rest,
　　And pass the heartless day.

" The sweeping blast, the sky o'ercast,"
　　The joyless winter day,
Let others fear, to me more dear
　　Than all the pride of May :
The tempest's howl, it soothes my soul,
　　My griefs it seems to join ;
The leafless trees my fancy please,
　　Their fate resembles mine !

Thou Power Supreme, whose mighty scheme
　　These woes of mine fulfil,
Here firm I rest—they must be best,
　　Because they are Thy will !
Then all I want, (oh ! do Thou grant
　　This one request of mine !)
Since to enjoy Thou dost deny.
　　Assist me to resign.　　　　　　*Burns.*

A WALK THROUGH VANITY FAIR.

SOME of the purchasers, I thought, made very foolish bargains. For instance, a young man, having inherited a splendid fortune, laid out a considerable portion of it in the purchase of diseases, and finally spent all the rest for a heavy lot of repentance and a suit of rags. A very pretty girl bartered a heart as clear as crystal, and which seemed her most valuable possession, for another jewel of the same kind, but so worn and defaced as to be utterly worthless. In one shop, there were a great many crowns of laurel and myrtle, which soldiers, authors, statesmen, and various other people, pressed eagerly to buy; some purchased these paltry wreaths with their lives; others by a toilsome servitude of years; and many sacrificed whatever was most valuable, yet finally slunk away without the crown. There was a sort of stock or scrip, called Conscience, which seemed to be in great demand, and would purchase almost anything. Indeed, few rich commodities were to be obtained without paying a heavy sum of this particular stock, and a man's business was seldom very lucrative, unless he knew precisely when and how to throw his hoard of Conscience into the market. Yet as this stock was the only thing of permanent value, whoever parted with it was sure to find himself a loser in the long run. Several of the speculations were of a questionable character. Occasionally, a member of parliament recruited his pocket by the sale of his constituents; and I was assured that public officers have often sold their country at very moderate prices. Thousands sold their happiness for a whim. Gilded chains were in great demand, and purchased with almost any sacrifice. In truth, those who desired, according to the old adage, to sell anything valuable for a song, might find customers all over the fair; and there were innumerable messes of pottage, piping hot, for such as chose to buy them with their birthrights. A few articles, however, could not be found genuine at Vanity Fair. If a customer wished to renew his stock of youth, the dealers offered him a set of false teeth and an auburn wig; if he demanded peace of mind, they recommended opium or a brandy-bottle.

Hawthorne.

THE CHILDREN'S HOUR.

BETWEEN the dark and the daylight,
    When the night is beginning to lower,
Comes a pause in the day's occupations,
    That is known as the Children's Hour.

I hear in the chamber above me
    The patter of little feet,
The sound of a door that is open'd,
    And voices soft and sweet.

From my study I see in the lamplight,
    Descending the broad hall-stair,
Grave Alice, and laughing Allegra,
    And Edith with golden hair.

A whisper, and then a silence :
  Yet I know by their merry eyes
They are plotting and planning together
  To take me by surprise.

A sudden rush from the stairway,
  A sudden raid from the hall !
By three doors left unguarded
  They enter my castle wall !

They climb up into my turret
  O'er the arms and back of my chair ;
If I try to escape they surround me :
  They seem to be everywhere.

They almost devour me with kisses,
  Their arms about me entwine,
Till I think of the Bishop of Bingen
  In his Mouse Tower on the Rhine !

Do you think, O blue-eyed banditti,
  Because you have scaled the wall,
Such an old moustache as I am
  Is not a match for you all !

I have you fast in my fortress,
  And will not let you depart,
But put you down into the dungeon
  In the round tower of my heart.

And there I will keep you for ever,
  Yes, for ever and a day,
Till the walls shall crumble to ruin,
  And moulder in dust away !

Longfellow.

THE POOR RELATION.

A POOR relation is the most irrelevant thing in nature, a piece of impertinent correspondency, an odious approximation, a haunting conscience, a preposterous shadow lengthening in the noontide of our prosperity, an unwelcome remembrancer, a perpetually-recurring mortification, a drain on your purse, a more intolerable dun upon your pride, a drawback upon success, a rebuke to your rising, a stain in your blood, a blot on your 'scutcheon, a rent in your garment, a death's head at your banquet, Agathocles's pot, a Mordecai in your gate, a Lazarus at your door, a lion in your path, a frog in your chamber, a fly in your ointment, a mote in your eye, a triumph to your enemy, an apology to your friends, the one thing not needful, the hail in harvest, the ounce of sour in a pound of sweet. He is known by his knock. Your heart telleth you, "That is Mr ——." A rap, between familiarity and respect, that demands, and at the same time seems to despair of entertainment. He entereth smiling and embarrassed. He holdeth out his hand to you to shake, and draweth it back again. He casually looketh in about dinner-time, when the table is full. He offereth to go away, seeing you have company, but is induced to stay. He filleth a chair, and your visitor's two children are accommodated at a side-table. He never cometh upon open days, when your wife says, with some complacency, "My dear, perhaps Mr —— will drop in to-day." He remembereth birthdays, and professeth he is fortunate to have stumbled upon one. He declareth against fish—the turbot being small—yet suffereth himself to be importuned into a slice against his first resolution. He sticketh by the port; yet will be prevailed upon to empty the remainder glass of claret, if a stranger press it upon him. He is a puzzle to the servants, who are fearful of being too obsequious, or not civil enough to him. The guests think "they have seen him before." Every one speculateth upon his condition; and the most part take him to be—a tide-waiter. He calleth you by your Christian name, to imply that his other is the same with your own. He is too familiar by half; yet you wish he had less diffidence. With half the familiarity, he might pass for a casual dependant; with more boldness, he would be in no danger of being taken for what he is. He is too humble for a friend; yet taketh on

him more state than befits a client. He is a worse guest than a country
tenant, inasmuch as he bringeth up no rent; yet 'tis odds, from his garb
and demeanour, that your guests take him for one. He is asked to make
one at the whist-table; refuseth on the score of poverty, and resents being
left out. When the company break up, he proffereth to go for a coach,
and lets the servant go. He recollects your grandfather; and will thrust
in some mean and quite unimportant anecdote of the family. He knew
it when it was not quite so flourishing as " he is blest in seeing it now."
He reviveth past situations, to institute what he calleth—favourable com-
parisons. With a reflecting sort of congratulation, he will inquire the
price of your furniture; and insults you with a special commendation of
your window curtains. He is of opinion that the urn is the more elegant
shape; but, after all, there was something more comfortable about the old
tea-kettle, which you must remember. He daresay you must find a great
convenience in having a carriage of your own, and appealeth to your lady
if it is not so. Inquireth if you have had your arms done on vellum yet;
and did not know, till lately, that such-and-such had been the crest of the
family. His memory is unseasonable; his compliments perverse; his talk
a trouble; his stay pertinacious; and when he goeth away, you dismiss
his chair into a corner as precipitately as possible, and feel fairly rid of
two nuisances.   *Lamb.*

A CLUSTER OF HEBREW PROVERBS.

IF any say, that one of thine ears is the ear of an ass, regard it not; if
he say so of them both, procure thyself a bridle.

That city is in a bad case whose physician hath the gout.

The camel, going to seek horns, lost his ears.

If a word be worth one shekel, silence is worth two.

When the weasel and the cat make a marriage, it is a very ill presage.

He that hath been bitten by a serpent is afraid of a rope.

He that hath had one of his family hanged, may not say to his neighbour, Hang up this fish.

They can find money for mischief who can find none to buy corn.

LONDON

HOUSES, churches, mix'd together;
  Streets, unpleasant in all weather;
Prisons, palaces, contiguous;
Gates, a bridge, the Thames irriguous;
Gaudy things enough to tempt you,
Showy outsides, insides empty;
Bubbles, trades, mechanic arts;
Coaches, wheelbarrows, and carts;
Warrants, bailiffs, bills unpaid,
Lords of laundresses afraid;
Rogues that nightly rob and shoot men,
Hangmen, aldermen, and footmen;
Lawyers, poets, priests, physicians,
Noble, simple—all conditions;

Worth, beneath a threadbare cover,
Villany, bedaub'd all over ;
Women, black, red, fair, and gray,
Prudes, and such as never pray,
Handsome, ugly, noisy, still,
Some that will not, some that will :
Many a beau without a shilling,
Many a widow not unwilling ;
Many a bargain if you strike it :
This is London—how d'ye like it !

A CLUSTER OF ENGLISH PROVERBS.

A BIT in the morning is better than nothing all day.
    Broken friendships may be soldered, but never sound.
He that buys a house that's wrought, hath many a pin and nail for nought.
Three may keep counsel, if two be away.
'Tis a good horse that never stumbles, and a good wife that never grumbles.
'Tis a long journey to the world's end.
Talk is but talk ; but 'tis money that buys land.
A man of courage never wants a weapon.
On the sea, sail ; on the land, settle.
Buying and selling is but winning and losing.
Every couple is not a pair.
Fetters of gold are fetters, and silken cords pinch.
Great pains and little gains soon make a man weary.
If young men had wit, and old men strength, all would be well.
That trial is not fair where affection is judge.
The king's cheese goes half away in parings.
Vows made in storms are forgotten in calms.
An ass that carries you is better than a horse that throws you.

COUNTRY HOSPITALITY.

AS soon as I entered the parlour, they put me into the great chair that
stood close by a huge fire, and kept me there by force until I was
almost stifled. Then a boy came in a great hurry to pull off my boots,
which I in vain opposed, urging that I must return soon after dinner. In
the meantime, the good lady whispered her eldest daughter, and slipped a
key into her hand; the girl returned instantly with a beer-glass half full of
aqua mirabilis and sirup of gillyflowers. I took as much as I had a mind
for, but madam vowed I should drink it off; for she was sure it would do
me good after coming out of the cold air; and I was forced to obey, which
absolutely took away my stomach. When dinner came in, I had a mind
to sit at a distance from the fire; but they told me it was as much as my
life was worth, and set me with my back just against it. Although my
appetite was quite gone, I was resolved to force down as much as I could,
and desired the leg of a pullet. "Indeed, Mr Bickerstaff," says the lady,
"you must eat a wing, to oblige me;" and so put a couple upon my plate.
I was persecuted at this rate during the whole meal: as often as I called
for small beer, the master tipped the wink, and the servant brought me a
brimmer of October.

Some time after dinner, I ordered my cousin's man, who came with me,
to get ready the horses; but it was resolved I should not stir that night;
and when I seemed pretty much bent upon going, they ordered the stable-
door to be locked, and the children hid my cloak and boots. The next
question was, What would I have for supper? I said, I never eat anything at night; but was at last, in my own defence, obliged to name the
first thing that came into my head. After three hours, spent chiefly in
apologies for my entertainment, insinuating to me, "That this was the
worst time of the year for provisions; that they were at a great distance
from any market; that they were afraid I should be starved; and that
they knew they kept me to my loss;" the lady went, and left me to her
husband; for they took special care I should never be alone. As soon
as her back was turned, the little misses ran backward and forward every
moment, and constantly as they came in, or went out, made a courtesy
directly at me, which, in good manners, I was forced to return with a
bow, and "your humble servant, pretty miss." Exactly at eight, the

mother came up, and discovered, by the redness of her face, that supper was not far off. It was twice as large as the dinner, and my persecution doubled in proportion. I desired at my usual hour to go to my repose, and was conducted to my chamber by the gentleman, his lady, and the whole train of children. They importuned me to drink something before I went to bed; and, upon my refusing, at last left a bottle of stingo, as they call it, for fear I should wake and be thirsty in the night.

I was forced in the morning to rise and dress myself in the dark, because they would not suffer my kinsman's servant to disturb me at the hour I desired to be called. I was now resolved to break through all measures to get away; and, after sitting down to a monstrous breakfast of cold beef, mutton, neat's tongues, venison pasty, and stale beer, took leave of the family. But the gentleman would needs see me part of the way, and carry me a short cut through his own ground, which he told me would save half a mile's riding. This last piece of civility had like to have cost me dear, being once or twice in danger of my neck by leaping over his ditches, and at last forced to alight in the dirt, when my horse, having slipped his bridle, ran away, and took us up more than an hour to recover him again. *Swift.*

BOOKS.

IN the best books, great men talk to us, give us their most precious thoughts, and pour their souls into ours. God be thanked for books! They are the voices of the distant and the dead, and make us heirs of the spiritual life of past ages. Books are the true levellers. They give to all who will faithfully use them, the society, the spiritual presence of the best and greatest of our race. No matter how poor I am—no matter though the prosperous of my own time will not enter my obscure dwelling—if the sacred writers will enter and take up their abode under my roof—if Milton will cross my threshold, and sing to me of paradise; and Shakespeare, to open to me the worlds of imagination, and the workings of the human heart; and Franklin, to enrich me with his practical wisdom I shall not pine for want of intellectual companionship; and I may become a culti vated man, though excluded from what is called the best society in the place where I live. *Channing.*

MODERN SPEAKING.

METHUSELAH might be half an hour in telling what o'clock it was; but as for us postdiluvians, we ought to do everything in haste; and in our speeches, as well as actions, remember that our time is short. A man that talks for a quarter of an hour together in company, if I meet him frequently, takes up a great part of my span. A quarter of an hour may be reckoned the eight-and-fortieth part of a day, a day the three hundred and sixtieth part of a year, and a year the threescore and tenth part of life.

I would establish but one great general rule to be observed in all conversation, which is this, " That men should not talk to please themselves, but those that hear them." This would make them consider whether what they speak be worth hearing; whether there be either wit or sense in what they are about to say; and whether it be adapted to the time when, the place where, and the person to whom, it is spoken. For the utter extirpation of these orators and story-tellers, which I look upon as very great pests of society, I have invented a watch which divides the minute into twelve parts, after the same manner that the ordinary watches are divided into hours; and will endeavour to get a patent, which shall oblige every club or company to provide themselves with one of these watches, that shall lie upon the table, as an hour-glass is often placed near the pulpit, to measure out the length of a discourse.

I shall be willing to allow a man one round of my watch, that is, a whole minute to speak in; but if he exceeds that time, it shall be lawful for any of the company to look upon the watch, or to call him down to order. Provided, however, that if any one can make it appear he is turned of threescore, he may take two, or, if he pleases, three rounds of the watch without giving offence. Provided also that this rule be not construed to extend to the fair sex, who shall still be at liberty to talk by the ordinary watch that is now in use. I would likewise earnestly recommend this little automaton, which may easily be carried in the pocket without any encumbrance, to all such as are troubled with this infirmity of speech, that upon pulling out their watches, they may have frequent occasion to consider what they are doing, and by that means cut the thread of the story short, and hurry to a conclusion.   *Steele.*

THE STRANGER.

A STRANGER came to a rich man's door,
And smiled on his mighty feast ;
And away his brightest child he bore,
And laid her toward the east.

He came next spring, with a smile as gay,
(At the time the east wind blows,)
And another bright creature he led away,
With a cheek like a burning rose.

And he came once more, when the spring was blue,
And whisper'd the last to rest,
And bore her away,—yet nobody knew
The name of the fearful guest !

Next year, there was none but the rich man left,—
Left alone in his pride and pain,
Who call'd on the stranger, like one bereft,
And sought through the land,—in vain !

He came not : he never was heard nor seen
Again, (so the story saith ;)
But wherever his terrible smile had been,
Men shudder'd, and talk'd of—Death !

Barry Cornwall.

THE GLOVE AND THE LIONS.

KING FRANCIS was a worthy king, and loved a royal sport,
     And one day, as his lions strove, sat looking on the court ;
The nobles fill'd the benches round, the ladies by their side,
And 'mongst them Count de Lorge, with one he hoped to make his bride :
And truly 'twas a gallant thing to see that crowning show,
Valour and love, and a king above, and the royal beasts below.

Ramp'd and roar'd the lions, with horrid laughing jaws,
They bit, they glared, gave blows like beams, a wind went with their paws ;
With wallowing might and stifled roar, they roll'd on one another,
Till all the pit, with sand and mane, was in a thund'rous smother ;
The bloody foam above the bars came whizzing through the air :
Said Francis then, " Good gentlemen, we 're better here than there !"

De Lorge's love o'erheard the king,—a beauteous, lively dame,
With smiling lips, and sharp bright eyes, which always seem'd the same :
She thought, " The Count, my lover, is as brave as brave can be :
He surely would do desperate things to show his love for me !
King, ladies, lovers, all look on ; the chance is wondrous fine ;
I 'll drop my glove to prove his love ; great glory will be mine !"

She dropp'd her glove to prove his love : then look'd on him and smiled :
He bow'd, and in a moment leap'd among the lions wild ;
The leap was quick ; return was quick ; he soon regain'd his place ;
Then threw the glove, but not with love, right in the lady's face ;
" In truth," cried Francis, " rightly done !" and he rose from where he sat :
" No love," quoth he, " but vanity, sets love a task like that !"

Leigh Hunt.

THE SHEPHERD BOY'S SONG.

H E that is down needs fear no fall ;
　　He that is low no pride ;
He that is humble ever shall
　　Have God to be his guide.

I am content with what I have,
　　Little be it or much ;
And, Lord ! contentment still I crave,
　　Because Thou savest such.

Fulness to such a burden is,
　　That go on pilgrimage ;
Here little, and hereafter bliss,
　　Is best from age to age.

Bunyan.

THE MOST TERRIFYING ADVENTURE OF THE WINDMILLS.

IN the midst of this their conversation, they discovered thirty or forty windmills all together on the plain, which the knight no sooner perceived than he said to his squire, " Chance has conducted our affairs even better than we could either wish or hope for : look there, friend Sancho, and behold thirty or forty outrageous giants, with whom I intend to engage in battle, and put every soul of them to death, so that we may begin to enrich ourselves with their spoils ; for it is a meritorious warfare, and serviceable both to God and man, to extirpate such a wicked race from the face of the earth." " What giants do you mean ?" said Sancho Panza, in amaze. " Those you see yonder," replied his master, " with vast extended arms, some of which are two leagues long." " I would your worship would take notice," replied Sancho, " that those you see yonder are no giants, but windmills ; and what seem arms to you are sails, which being turned with the wind, make the mill-stone work." " It seems very plain," said the knight, " that you are but a novice in adventures ; these I affirm to be giants, and if thou art afraid, get out of the reach of danger, and put up thy prayers for me, while I join with them in fierce and unequal combat." So saying, he put spurs to his steed Rozinante, without paying the least regard to the cries of his squire Sancho, who assured him that those he was going to attack were not giants, but innocent windmills ; but he was so much possessed with the opinion that they were giants, that he neither heard the advice of his squire Sancho, nor would use the intelligence of his own eyes, though he was very near them : on the contrary, when he approached them he called aloud, " Fly not, ye base and cowardly miscreants, for he is but a single knight who now attacks you." At that instant, a breeze of wind springing up, the great sails began to turn, which being perceived by Don Quixote, " Though you wield," said he, " more arms than ever belonged to the giant Briareus, I will make you pay for your insolence." So saying, and heartily recommending himself to his lady Dulcinea, whom he implored to succour him in this emergency, bracing on his target, and setting his lance in the rest, he put his Rozinante to full speed, and assaulting the nearest windmill, thrust it into one of the sails,

which was driven about by the wind with so much fury, that the lance was shivered to pieces, and both knight and steed whirled aloft, and overthrown in very bad plight upon the plain.

Sancho Panza rode as fast as the ass could carry him to his assistance, and when he came up found him unable to stir, by reason of the bruises which he and Rozinante had received. " Lord have mercy upon us !" said the squire, " did not I tell your worship to consider well what you were about? Did I not assure you they were no other than windmills? Indeed, nobody could mistake them for anything else, but one who has windmills in his own head." " Prithee, hold thy peace, friend Sancho," replied Don Quixote ; " the affairs of war are more than anything subject to change. How much more so, as I believe, nay, am certain, that the sage Freston, who stole my closet and books, has converted those giants into mills, in order to rob me of the honour of their overthrow, such is the enmity he bears me ; but in the end all his treacherous arts will but little avail against the vigour of my sword." " God's will be done !" replied Sancho Panza, who helped him to rise and mount Rozinante, that was almost disjointed. *Don Quixote.*

POETRY.

POETRY is, as was said more than two thousand years ago, imitation. It is an art analogous in many respects to the art of painting, sculpture, and acting. The imitations of the painter, the sculptor, and the actor, are indeed, within certain limits, more perfect than those of the poet. The machinery which the poet employs consists merely of words; and words cannot, even when employed by such an artist as Homer or Dante, present to the mind images of visible objects quite so lively and exact as those which we carry away from looking on the works of the brush and the chisel. But, on the other hand, the range of poetry is infinitely wider than that of any other imitative art, or than that of all the other imitative arts together. The sculptor can imitate only form; the painter only form and colour; the actor, until the poet supplies him with words, only form, colour, and motion. Poetry holds the outer world in common with the other arts. The heart of man is the province of poetry, and of poetry alone. The painter, the sculptor, and the actor can exhibit no more of human passion and character than that small portion which overflows into the gesture and the face, always an imperfect, often a deceitful, sign of that which is within. The deeper and more complex parts of human nature can be exhibited by means of words alone. Thus the objects of the imitation of poetry are the whole external and the whole internal universe, the face of nature, the vicissitudes of fortune, man as he is in himself, man as he appears in society, all things which really exist, all things of which we can form an image in our minds by combining together parts of things which really exist. The domain of this imperial art is commensurate with the imaginative faculty.

Macaulay.

BALLANTYNE AND COMPANY, PRINTERS, EDINBURGH AND LONDON.

NIMMO'S CARMINE GIFT-BOOKS.

Small 4to, beautifully printed within red lines on superior paper, handsomely bound in cloth extra, bevelled boards, gilt edges, price 7s. 6d.,

ROSES AND HOLLY:

A Gift-Book for all the Year. With Original Illustrations by GOURLAY STEELL, R.S.A.; SAM. BOUGH, A.R.S.A.; JOHN M'WHIRTER; R. HERDMAN, R.S.A.; CLARK STANTON, A.R.S.A.; J. LAWSON; and other eminent Artists.

'This is really a collection of art and literary gems—the prettiest book, take it all in all, that we have seen this season.'—*Illustrated Times.*

Uniform with the above, price 7s. 6d.,

PEN AND PENCIL PICTURES FROM THE POETS.

A Series of Forty beautiful Illustrations on Wood, with Descriptive Selections from the Writings of the Poets, elegantly printed within red lines, on superfine paper.

Uniform with the above, price 7s. 6d.,

GEMS OF LITERATURE:

Elegant, Rare, and Suggestive. A Collection of the most notable Beauties of the English Language, appropriately Illustrated with upwards of One Hundred Original Engravings, drawn expressly for this work. Beautifully printed within red lines, on superfine paper.

'For really luxurious books, Nimmo's "Pen and Pencil Pictures from the Poets" and "Gems of Literature" may be well recommended. They are luxurious in the binding, in the print, in the engravings, and in the paper.'—*Morning Post.*

Uniform with the above, price 7s. 6d,

THE BOOK OF ELEGANT EXTRACTS.

Profusely Illustrated by the most eminent Artists. Choicely printed on superfine paper, within red lines.

Nimmo's Popular Edition of the Works of the Poets.

In fcap. 8vo, printed on toned paper, elegantly bound in cloth extra, gilt edges, price 3s. 6d. each; or in morocco antique, price 6s. 6d. each. Each Volume contains a Memoir, and is illustrated with a Portrait of the Author, engraved on Steel, and numerous full-page Illustrations on Wood, from designs by eminent Artists.

LONGFELLOW'S POETICAL WORKS.
SCOTT'S POETICAL WORKS.
BYRON'S POETICAL WORKS.
MOORE'S POETICAL WORKS.
WORDSWORTH'S POETICAL WORKS.
COWPER'S POETICAL WORKS.
MILTON'S POETICAL WORKS.
THOMSON'S POETICAL WORKS.
BEATTIE AND GOLDSMITH'S POETICAL WORKS.
POPE'S POETICAL WORKS.
BURNS'S POETICAL WORKS.
THE CASQUET OF GEMS:
A Volume of Choice Selections from the Works of the Poets.

UNIFORM IN APPEARANCE AND PRICE.

THE COMPLETE WORKS OF SHAKESPEARE.
With BIOGRAPHICAL SKETCH by MARY COWDEN CLARKE. Two Volumes, price 3s. 6d. each.

THE ARABIAN NIGHTS ENTERTAINMENTS.
With One Hundred Illustrations on Wood. Two Volumes, price 3s. 6d. each.

BUNYAN'S PILGRIM'S PROGRESS AND HOLY WAR.
Complete in One Volume.

LIVES OF THE BRITISH POETS:
BIOGRAPHIES of the most eminent British Poets, with Specimens of their Writings. Twelve Portraits on Steel, and Twelve full-page Illustrations.

EDINBURGH: WILLIAM P. NIMMO.

AND SOLD BY ALL BOOKSELLERS.